The Shadow
of Seth

Books by Tom Llewellyn

The Tilting House
The Shadow of Seth

The Shadow of Seth

Tom Llewellyn

The Poisoned Pencil

An imprint of Poisoned Pen Press

Copyright © 2015 by Tom Llewellyn

First Edition 2015

10 9 8 7 6 5 4 3 2 1

Library of Congress Catalog Card Number: 2014958042

ISBN: 9781929345182   Trade Paperback
        9781929345199   E-book

The Poisoned Pencil
An imprint of Poisoned Pen Press
6962 E. First Ave., Ste. 103
Scottsdale, AZ 85251
www.thepoisonedpencil.com
info@thepoisonedpencil.com

Printed in the United States of America

This one's for the boys:
Ben and Abel Llewellyn

Acknowledgments

Thanks to my talented editor at The Poisoned Pencil, Ellen Larson, for loving YA mysteries and liking this one enough to introduce it to the world. Thanks to my agent, the esteemed Abigail Samoun, for knocking on doors until Ellen finally answered. Thanks to Ben Llewellyn for helping me create Seth's soundtrack. Thanks to Sweet Pea Flaherty, for being a character in real life and for loaning his name to a character in this book. Thanks to my dear friend Lance Kagey for lending his design talent to the cover. And finally, thanks to my beloved city of Tacoma, for letting me set a murder within its city limits.

One

Nadel called my cell phone just as I got home from school, asking if I could make a pickup. Mom was sleeping. She wouldn't need her car until she left for work, after dinner. I took her car keys and drove her Jeep over to Nadel's House of Clocks.

Nadel was in the workshop behind the showroom. He had thick, magnifying glasses strapped to his mostly bald head and was bent over a vise, filing a groove into a steel rod the size of a pencil. The shop smelled like iron filings and machine oil.

"That you, Seth?"

"Hey, Mr. Nadel. What're you working on?"

"An old Waltham wall clock. Eight-day regulator. Not worth the price of the repair, but the lady said it has sentimental value." Nadel had lived in the States for forty years, but his German accent was still heavy. "Sentimental to her, maybe. To me, its value is rent money."

"You wanted me to pick something up?"

"Yes, the address is there on the workbench, by the drill press."

I found a scrap of paper with the name Lear and an Old Town address on it. A nice neighborhood.

Nadel looked at me with a tilt of his head. "They had their maid call. Real Richie Rich types, so use your manners when you go."

Nadel paid me twenty bucks for a pickup or delivery. It was easy money. Nadel didn't like driving, so he was as happy to pay it as a miser like him could stand to be. I drove from his shop to Heath Way, took a left before I reached the high school, and followed Tacoma Avenue past the Lawn and Tennis Club.

The Lear house was set far back from the road. It had a lawn big enough to land a small plane on and came complete with water features and statues of children playing—statues as nice to look at as real kids, but without all that annoying life and breath.

I climbed about one hundred steps to the front door, then lifted the heavy knocker and let it fall. A Latino woman in a starched white uniform opened the door.

"Are you for the clock?" Her accent was Mexican, but more *carne asada* than taco truck.

"I'm for it, if you are."

She gestured to come inside. "Please."

"Thank you." We had all the politeness covered and she walked across an entryway about the size of my high school gym. I could hear her shoes echo down a hallway and hoped she'd come back sometime that day.

I looked around. The entryway ceiling must have been twenty feet high. A huge crystal chandelier hung halfway down, but the only light came from an arched doorway that led into another room. Peeking around that doorway was a sliver of a girl's face. All I could see was an eye and a waterfall of dark brown hair, but if the rest of the face matched, it was probably lovely.

"Nice place you have here," I said to the face.

The face stepped into sight, followed by a body that was equally lovely, dressed in a black tank top and a short denim skirt. It was a body that kept in shape playing on elite soccer teams and dancing with honor students. I'd seen her before at school—she wasn't the type you forget—but I didn't know her name. She hung around the rich kids. If I remembered correctly, she spent a lot of time on the arm of Erik Jorgenson, one of the Heath High royalty.

"Yeah, real homey," said the girl, in a voice that surprised me with its hint of roughness, as if she'd yelled too much as a kid. "You can hear your echo, because it's that big and empty. I'll trade you anytime."

"If you saw my apartment, I don't think you would."

"You have an apartment? Where?"

I laughed. "I'm not telling you where I live. People from your part of town can't be trusted."

"You don't really have an apartment, do you?"

"You say *apartment* like it's something exotic. It's a room with a bed in it."

"Sounds dangerous. Tell me where it is."

I gave in. "You drive your daddy's BMW down K Street until it crosses Division and the street name changes to Martin Luther King Jr. Way. That's how you know you've entered my neighborhood. They don't honor Martin on your block, because it's bad for property values. You keep driving until you pass Hilltop Pawn Shop. On the next block, you'll see a big red sign that says Boxing. Click your remote until the alarm chirps, then go inside the boxing gym. When ChooChoo and the other men in there see someone who looks like you, they might teach you a few new words, but just ignore them. Head all the way to the back, by the rusty boiler, and go up the stairway there until you come to the only door. That's the door to my home. Kitchen, bed, and TV all in one handy room. The whole place would probably fit in your bathtub."

Her big eyes opened even wider. "How old are you?" she asked.

"Old enough. Sixteen."

"Me, too. I've seen you before. You go to Heath High, don't you?

"Yes. Look, I got things to do. Any chance you could help the *señora* find the clock so I can get out of here?"

She didn't move, except to stick out her bottom lip.

"What's your name?"

"Seth."

"That's right. Seth. And you have a funny last name, if I remember right. What're you doing this Friday?"

"Why? You need someone to mow your lawn?"

"I'm going to a party, and Janine would totally flip over you."

"Yeah, that's my job. To make Janine flip. Look, umm—"

"—Azura—" She seemed suddenly self-conscious when she said her name, bringing her chin down so that she looked at me through her eyelashes.

"Azura? Azura Lear? Sounds like a brand of luggage. Look, Azura, I've never been very good at parties. I think I'll just take the clock and go home, if that's all right with you."

"It's not." She got up and walked slowly away, sashaying her denim skirt back and forth as she went, leaving me in the faintest wake of a soft perfume. She was like a walking permission slip. She turned once when she reached the hallway and tapped her finger on her lips. I couldn't tell if she was trying to think of something to say or asking me to keep quiet. She turned away again and sashayed out of sight.

The housekeeper came back with a cardboard box containing the clock. I left, giving her a *Gracias, señora,* just to show off my bilingual skills.

Two

Nadel was still bent over the tiny metal rod, filing away, when I came in with the box. Mom had been cleaning his shop since I was a baby. When she first started, she worked in the daytime and often brought me with her. Nadel complained at the beginning. "*Fraulein*, this is no place for babies. All the parts for choking. And baby noise is a noise I cannot work around." But Mom explained that I was a different kind of kid. I kept quiet and wouldn't get into things.

Mom told me that I used to sit and watch Nadel work for hours without making a sound. Pretty soon, Nadel was giving me oily tools to play with and letting me dig through boxes of broken mainsprings and worn-out escapement gears. By the time I was in third grade, I could fix most simple pendulum clocks, with a little help from Nadel.

Nadel taught me that many things people think are fragile, like antique clocks, are actually pretty tough. And almost everything can be fixed. "My customers—they should be careful. If they break it, it costs them money. But me, I shouldn't worry about careful. If I break it, I fix what I break and charge them extra." Nadel knew he could fix anything. So I smiled when he grabbed the box from me and set it on his workbench with a clunk, as if it contained a piece of scrap metal instead of an antique.

"How was the house?"

"Big."

"Who answered the door?"

"The maid."

Nadel nodded. He opened the box and hauled out a pendulum wall clock, about three feet long and shaped like a chunky banjo. "An old one," he said, walking his fingers along the burled wood of the case. "Early 1800s or even late 1700s. A Simon Willard—see the signature? Look at the joints. Perfect. And gold-plating, though it's mostly worn off the lens frame. Wonder if they want me to replate it." Nadel could do anything required to fix a clock. With his store of chemicals and the skills of a metallurgist, he could restore the gold or silver-plating on a clock face. With the hands of a machinist, he could craft steel parts from scratch. He hung the clock from a peg on the wall, leveled it with a practiced squint, opened the case, and gave the pendulum a swing. It swung once and stopped.

Nadel pulled the clock off the wall and laid it facedown on a shop towel. The back of the beautiful old clock was as plain and unvarnished as the underside of a kitchen table. Nadel casually pried a panel off the back with a screwdriver and looked inside. He frowned, then pulled out a crumpled, folded, yellowed piece of paper. "Rich people using a clock case as a recycle bin." He tossed the paper toward a distant trashcan and only barely missed. Without replacing the panel, he hung the clock back on the wall and gave the pendulum a swing. The clock ticked happily away.

"That didn't take long. You want me to bring it back to the Richie Rich house?" If I had to, I figured, I could force myself to see that girl again.

Nadel scowled. "Are you crazy? Maybe in a week you'll bring it back. Maybe two weeks. Lear can afford more than fifteen minutes of my time, Seth. And this clock is worth a hefty bill. A maid who answers the door? A Simon Willard? I'm trying to keep open my business and you want to bring the clock back in fifteen minutes?"

I left Nadel to his creative invoicing. I walked through the ticks and tocks of his showroom and drove the six blocks to Shotgun Shack for a bite to eat. "Oh My" by Sweatshop Union had played only halfway through when I parked, but the song was so good I had to sit and listen to the whole thing.

We need food, clothes, and shelter,
So we hustle till we're old and helpless,
And if you do only go for the gold and wealth,
You're still alone 'cause you don't know yourself…

By the time the song ended, my mouth was watering for Miss Irene's cornbread stuffing. I walked inside the restaurant. Mismatched wooden tables were carefully arranged by Miss Irene to fit in as many customers as possible. A good thing, since Shotgun Shack was standing-room-only most nights and weekend mornings. The black-and-white linoleum floor was worn but clean. A counter was faced by a row of bar stools. Behind the counter stood Checker Cab, a big, soft, black man whose mouth hung open, even though he always breathed loudly through his nose.

It was mid-afternoon, so the restaurant was mostly empty. Stanley Chang, an old Hawaiian whose full legal name was about a million syllables long, sat at his booth by the front door, pouring over a battered copy of the *Tacoma News Tribune*. Stanley Chang wore colorful silk shirts, even if the rest of his clothes were old and worn. Today he had on a dark red shirt with gold leaf patterns on it. It didn't match the tweed sports coat he wore over the top of it, but, man, that shirt was sure something. The jacket was too small for Stanley's big belly, but that put more of the beautiful shirt on display.

Stanley Chang said he came to Shotgun Shack for the catfish and greens, but no one believed him. Southern soul food was never real big in Honolulu, where Stanley grew up. Everyone knew that what really brought Stanley there were his feelings for Miss Irene. Stanley Chang was sweeter on Miss Eye than the cane syrup on her corncakes. She'd come over to his table—she waited on him personally whenever she could—and he'd straighten the collar of his shirt and say, "Mahalo, Ko`u Ku`u Lei" in a slow island drawl. And she would giggle and say, "Stanley Chang, you better cut out that tropical talking or I might just accidentally fall in your lap." She'd laugh, but Stanley would just stare at her with his dark, hungry eyes.

Back in the corner, King George talked loudly into his cell phone. George was only a year older than me, but seemed to take up twice as much space. Back in middle school, he'd been something like a myth used to scare sixth graders. *You'd better be cool,* an eighth grader might have said, *or King George will murder you on your way home.* And he really might have. George had been in and out of juvie at least three times that I could remember.

King George had dropped out of school when he was fourteen. Nowadays, he always had a roll of cash as big as a fist jammed into his pocket. If anyone ever asked where he got it, King George would just give them The Look and they would stop asking. The Look said, "Ask me again, and I will inflict great pain on your body."

I figured Miss Irene must be particularly scared of George, even though George was only seventeen. She complained about him constantly and quietly back in the kitchen, but she let him hang out in the restaurant as long as he wanted, even when ten customers were waiting for a seat.

As far as I could tell, King George only did three things: sat in Shotgun Shack eating rib-eye steaks, lifted weights to keep his arms as big as my legs, and rode around town on his black BMX bike. He couldn't get his license until he turned eighteen, because he'd never gone to driving school. For a while, he'd driven around a black Lincoln SUV, but the cops had pulled him over a couple of times and finally impounded the car. King George made that BMX bike look small.

At Shotgun Shack, King George would shout his meat orders across the restaurant. "Miss Irene! I want me a rib-eye and a brisket!"

"What you want to drink?"

"I *want* a protein shake, but since that seems to be too complicated, get me a black coffee and a glass of milk."

"You should eat a salad or some fresh fruit," Stanley Chang would say, glancing over the top of his newspaper. "All that meat and no roughage plug you up."

"You better shut up, old man, or you gonna feature prominently in my evening workout." Stanley, who was probably fifty years old, would duck behind his newspaper like a kid playing peek-a-boo and King George would grumble and fuss until a few pounds of meat were set in front of him.

That day, when I walked in, Stanley Chang said, "*Aloha, makamaka.* How are you today?"

"Hey, Stanley."

"That Seth?" shouted Miss Irene from the kitchen. "Slugger, come on back here and help me fill an order or two."

I'd always loved cooking with Miss Irene. Mom had never cooked much, but hanging with Miss Eye in her kitchen felt like mom-time to me, even if we were cooking for customers instead of family. Miss Eye said I was a natural in the kitchen. I liked the process of cooking. Order mattered. Amounts mattered.

Miss Irene acted like she needed my help, even though I knew she worked faster when I wasn't there. I'd been cooking on that grill and in those fryers for quite a few years, but I still couldn't keep up with the movements of Miss Eye. Every motion of her hand accomplished something. She could crack an egg and separate the yolk from the white with one hand, dumping the white into a bowl for a lemon meringue pie and using the yolks for an egg wash for her fried chicken.

She told me to clean my hands, then asked me to mix up her secret seasoning salt with some flour, garlic powder, and black pepper. I measured the ingredients and stirred them together with my still-damp fingers, the white flour filling in the cracks of my knuckles. Once I was done, I started dipping chicken parts into the egg wash, then coated them carefully in the flour mixture, then back in the eggs, then back in the flour and into the fryer basket.

"How was school today?" asked Miss Irene, as she checked on her beans and cornbread. She asked to make sure I'd actually gone. I usually did. I was a decent student. Mostly B's. A few A's. And a C here and there just to add a little flavor.

"Same o same o."

"Mmm-hmmm. How's your mom?"

"You know how she is. She's in here every night, Miss Eye."

"She was surely in here last night. She was madder 'n ever at me. I meant how is she today?"

"Haven't seen her yet. She was asleep when I left. Why? What happened?"

"The same and more of it. Thought we was gonna come to blows."

"And that's okay with you, even if you're paying her?"

"I will admit—I'm tired of it. There are times when I wish she'd just leave and never come back."

"Careful what you wish for. She tends to disappear enough as it is."

"But she always shows up for work. Slugger, that woman never missed a night of work that I can remember. No matter what you think of her, she's always worked hard. "

"Yeah, as a cleaning lady."

"You watch it, son. She's kept a roof over your head, such as it is."

"Yeah, such as it is."

"Last night we had more words than usual. I might have actually said something about not wanting her back. She might have said something about not coming back. Honestly, I'm not really sure. I hope she comes in tonight, but I might have fired her. Or she might have quit."

"Appreciate the clarity."

"Chicken's getting brown."

Mom and Miss Irene had known each other for decades. They used to be like sisters—one white and one black. Miss Irene respected my mom for being such a hard worker and for cleaning her restaurant better than anyone else could. Customers would comment about how clean everything was and Miss Irene would say, "That's because I got me the best cleaning woman in all of Tacoma." Some of those customers even hired my mom to start cleaning their businesses or houses, too.

Miss Irene also used to talk about how she liked Mom's wild side. When Mom would blow a paycheck on something frivolous—a dinner at Primo Grill or a new Stetson for ChooChoo, Miss Eye would say, "She's a free spirit. When she ain't cleaning, she does what she wants without thinking about tomorrow." But she'd say it with sadness in her voice, because she knew when Mom blew a whole paycheck on a single meal, that meant Mom and I would be counting on food banks and handouts to feed us for the next two weeks. And Miss Eye also knew that sometimes Mom blew our rent money on darker stuff.

Then, six months ago, Mom came into Shotgun Shack, right before closing, to start cleaning. A few minutes earlier, Checker Cab had dropped a plate of pork chops in the kitchen doorway. He'd picked up the food, but left the grease there. When Mom stepped on that grease spot, her feet went out from under her. On the way down, she hit her head on the edge of a table and broke a front tooth in half. When she saw herself in the mirror, she was mad. That front tooth was right in the middle of her smile. She and Miss Irene and Checker got in a shouting match over who was going to pay for that tooth. Mom and Miss Eye haven't talked much since, except to yell at each other.

I pulled out the chicken and let the hot oil drip. Then I dumped the chicken into a basket lined with wax paper. Miss Eye scooped a serving of macaroni and cheese and nestled it next to the chicken. She set the basket on the sill of the window to the dining room and hit the bell. "Order up." From the other side of the window, Checker Cab grabbed the basket of chicken and walked sleepily toward a waiting diner.

All the customers were fed, so I made chicken for Miss Irene and myself. We ate it in the kitchen. Miss Irene would never let the help be seen eating in front of customers. She said it was *unsightly*. While I was eating, I asked Miss Eye if she wanted me to stick around for the dinner crowd that was less than an hour away, thinking maybe it would help patch things up between Mom and Miss Eye, but she said she and Checker had it covered.

"Not sure what you see in that guy, Miss Eye." I nodded in Checker's direction.

"He may not be the fastest worker around," she said, "but he gets it done. Eventually."

The story was that Miss Eye had first hired Checker years ago, when he was little more than a chubby street kid hanging around looking for free food. According to my mom, nobody really knew why she had taken him on, but he'd been at Shotgun Shack so long, he was as much a part of it as the Open sign. It always seemed to me that Miss Eye was half Checker's employer and half his mother.

I went home, thinking how that chicken felt good in my stomach, thinking how happy my mouth was. I could still taste the grease and garlic in the corners of my lips.

I thought about Azura, too. It surprised me that she came forward from the back room of my brain, but there she was. I could see those big eyes peeking around the doorway. I could smell the hint of perfume that brushed the air when she left the room. I was still thinking about her when I walked through the door of ChooChoo's boxing gym.

ChooChoo had been Mom's off-and-on boyfriend for the last decade. Years ago, ChooChoo converted a crappy, second-story storeroom into a crappy, second-story apartment. Mom and I had moved in and out of that apartment half a dozen times since she first met ChooChoo. When they first decided they were in love, we left behind the motel room we were living in down on Pacific Avenue and moved into the gym apartment. Six months later, they got in a fight when

ChooChoo thought Mom was flirting with one of the train-ers. Mom and I moved back into the motel. Then ChooChoo grew lonely and they made up. We moved back in. He'd grow jealous again and back to the motel we'd go. They'd make up. We'd move back. They'd fight. Out we'd go.

Still, that gym was what I thought of as home. I didn't think of ChooChoo as my dad, but he was okay to me most of the time. His temper sat right on the edge of his brain and he could lose it at the smallest things. When he did, his dump-truck shoulders and boulder-sized fists would scare the breath out of me. He never hit me, but I thought he was going to a few times. Then a gentle mood would wash over him and he'd become as soft and safe as a stuffed animal.

On my seventh birthday, which happened during a time when he and mom were all huggy and kissy, he bought me a pair of bright red Everlast boxing gloves. They were youth sized, but still too big for me. I loved those gloves. I ate my birthday cake with them on and slept in them that night. In the morning, my hands were pruny from sweat.

Later that same day, ChooChoo started teaching me how to box. When he bought the gloves, I think he figured he'd turn his true love's only son into a boxing legend, like he used to be. He hefted me up into the ring and started showing me how to hold my hands. I picked up the basics instantly. "Lookit th' stance o' this kid," he'd say, proudly. "Lookit how 'e bobs but still keeps 'is chin tucked in." When ChooChoo talked, his words ran together. He left out every letter he could get away with. I figured it was because he talked like he boxed—fluid and fast.

I've always had a perfect stance. About two years ago, ChooChoo was training a fighter who went by the pro name of Hector Heat. Hector was a brawler who could take a punch and shrug it off. But he stood in the ring like an overweight cop. One day, when Hector was sparring, ChooChoo yelled at me, "Seth! Come over here an' show this kid how t'stand!" Hector Heat stared at my skinny arms and bony chest and started laughing. ChooChoo slapped Hector so hard on the back of the head that he knocked him straight to the mat. "Don' choo laugh at this boy 'ntil you getta decent stance y'self."

I never developed the muscle to be a real fighter. And I never developed the quickness. ChooChoo realized this in less than a year. But he kept teaching me. He'd say, "Y' got th' sense for it—jus' ain't got th' body." Still, all those lessons kept me from getting beat up too badly on the walk home from school. I got in my share of fights, but I won enough to earn some neighborhood respect. And it probably didn't hurt to be living above the business of one of the biggest, scariest men on the Hilltop.

When I walked in, ChooChoo was in the ring buckling headgear on a couple of young fighters. "Now I tol' you," he said to the bigger one, "y' got t' change things up. Y' can't throw a cross after ev'ry two jabs. Y' got to wait fo' yer opp'tunity." The kid nodded. ChooChoo hit him playfully on the side of the head and the two young men started boxing.

I walked over to the ring. "Hey, Chooch."

"'Sup, Seth?"

"Big one's your prospect, huh?"

ChooChoo nodded and sipped coffee from a Styrofoam cup, grimacing with each sip. "A.J. can punch like a jackhammer. But I can a'ready tell he ain't gon' cut it. One round and Li'l Ronny a'ready got 'is number."

The two boxers circled each other. Little Ronny was a good twenty pounds lighter than A.J., but he was quick. He danced around the ring, shuffling his feet back and forth. A.J. kept following Ronny with his eyes, but wasn't close enough to hit him. Little Ronny moved in and started jabbing away at A.J. and A.J. took the punches. Then he jabbed with his left. Ronny bobbed out of the way. A.J. jabbed again, then threw a right cross, but only hit air. He jabbed again, then again, then threw another right cross. This time, Ronny ducked the cross and threw a vicious counterpunch, hitting A.J.'s unprotected chin right on the nut. A.J.'s head snapped back. Ronny hit him again, then again. A.J. fell to the mat.

"Maybe Little Ronny is your real prospect."

"Maybe. Small but smart, eh?" ChooChoo grunted as he pulled himself into the ring to tend to A.J. I walked through the gym to the back stairs, which led up to our apartment.

I opened the door. Mom was sleeping on the daybed in the corner. I plunked onto the couch and turned the TV on, volume down low. I watched the early news for a few minutes. A Seattle cop had killed a homeless guy. A New York congressman was caught in an investment scandal. The house fires in Centralia looked like arson. I flipped the TV off, went to the kitchen table, and thumbed through today's stack of mail.

The envelope was third from the top. Pale blue, like always. No return address, like always. This time the postmark said St. Louis, Missouri. Did that mean he was living in St. Louis again?

I tore open the envelope and removed the money. Five fifty-dollar bills, just like every month for as long as I could remember. On the top bill was a yellow sticky-note. Plain, block letters said, "The world is dirty, so what's the point of staying clean?"

What the hell was that supposed to mean?

I opened the fridge. In the back was a yellow Gold'n Soft margarine tub. Mom didn't trust banks, so this was where we

kept our savings. I pulled off the lid and pulled out the rest of
the money. There was four hundred and thirty dollars inside. I
added the two-fifty, bringing our total savings to six hundred
and eighty dollars.

"That you, hon'?"

"Hi, Mom."

"Hi, baby. How was school?"

"I did all right on my history test."

"Knew you would, honey. Anything else?"

"After school I ran an errand for Nadel. Did a little cooking with Miss Irene."

Mom was quiet for a while, then said, "That's fine."

I nodded toward the refrigerator. "The envelope came
from the mystery man." She smiled, but was looking across
the room, staring at nothing. She did this when she was upset
about something. It was her version of crying. "What's wrong?
What happened?" I asked, even though I knew the answer.

"Oh, nothing you need to worry about."

I sighed. "That means there's something I need to worry
about. What?"

"No you don't need to. It's nothing. Never had a problem
finding work. I can just get another customer. Most everyone
needs something cleaned. There's some leftover pizza in the
fridge."

"I already ate. I talked to Miss Eye. She wants to work it
out with you."

"Not this time. I'm done with that place. That woman.
What time is it?"

"Five."

"I've got to go to work. I'll go and clean for her at least
one more time. And the rest of my customers still want toilets
scrubbed." She rolled onto her feet and kissed me on the cheek.

Her breath smelled sour and there were dark circles under her eyes. "I bought you a new pair of shoes. At the end of the bed."

"You bought shoes on the same day you lost a customer? Mom, you two got to work things out."

She ignored me and pointed toward the shoes. "I think you'll like them. Try them on while I take a shower."

Mom had four cleaning customers right now, if Shotgun Shack still counted. Trinity Presbyterian Church, where she vacuumed up fishy crackers crushed into the carpet by the after-school kids. Pastor Vandegrift was a hard guy to read, but had always been nice to Mom and me. Allied Allstar Drivers' Academy was a new customer. I'd never met the man who ran that place. The other two were Nadel and Miss Irene.

I picked up the shoes.

Most of my clothes come from two places: the Goodwill or the clothing bank at Trinity Church. It sucked, but I wasn't the only kid in town who dressed that way. "Tacoma is a good place to be poor," Mom liked to say. But we've always spent money on my shoes. In my neighborhood, it didn't matter so much what a sixteen-year-old boy wore from the ankles up. I tended toward baggy jeans from Goodwill and tight, white tank tops I bought at K-Mart. But your shoes were a sign of your status—that you either mattered to someone or to no one.

Mom knew it. She'd never complained when I'd drop one hundred and twenty dollars on a pair of high-tops, even though that was money we needed for rent and food. I opened the box and saw a beautiful pair of black-on-black Nike LeBrons. Last time I checked, they were one-forty. But they were worth it to me, because LeBron was The Man and just his name made the shoes cool. I laced them up and put them on.

Mom came out of the bathroom dressed for work in faded blue Dickies, a man's white dress shirt, and a pair of old sneakers. "How do you like them?" She smiled toward my new shoes, broken tooth and all.

"You shouldn't have bought them. You know we can't afford them. Rent's due in just a couple of days."

"We can't afford a lot of things, Seth, but that doesn't mean we shouldn't have them."

"Yeah, I've heard that one before."

"Well, you're welcome. I gotta go. You on your own for the rest of the night?"

"Yup. Alone and out of trouble."

"Come give me a kiss good-bye."

I kissed her on the cheek, then hugged her. She smelled like bleach. Like the work she did to keep me clothed and fed. "Thanks for the shoes. I do love them."

"Not as much as I love you, hon. Be good."

She left. It was the last time I'd ever see her alive.

Three

I spent the evening dozing in and out of TV shows, instead of doing my history homework. We were supposed to be reading about Lyndon Johnson and the Vietnam War, but I was two chapters behind. It was a few minutes after nine o'clock when I heard a knock on the apartment door. I yelled, "Come in," because I figured it was ChooChoo letting me know he was going home. The door opened and a rough female voice said, "Your directions were exactly right."

Azura was inside my apartment and closing the door behind her. Her big eyes made the room look small and her fine clothes made it look shabby. I jumped up to my feet and said, "What are you doing here?"

"I came to see you."

"I don't think I know you well enough to have you in my home."

"You were in mine. And you're the one who told me how to get here. You wouldn't have told me if you didn't want me to come."

"Don't go all psychology on me. I was in your entryway. You're in my bedroom." I pushed her back out the door and closed it behind me.

"Hey!" said Azura. She stepped away from me. "You're not being nice."

"Welcome to the neighborhood." I wanted to kick her all the way out of the gym. I wanted to do other things, too. "Can we at least go somewhere else?"

She nodded toward the door. "My car's outside."

We walked downstairs. ChooChoo and his friend, a trainer named Manny, were the only ones still in the gym. Manny whistled, but ChooChoo cuffed him on the ear. "Don't tease the kid, Manny," ChooChoo said. "He doesn't get many girls in here. Especially ones that look like that. Damn, Seth." Azura smiled nervously.

Outside was a black Lexus coupe. Not a BMW maybe, but awful close.

"This is yours, isn't it?" I said, running my fingers along a shiny fender.

She chirped the doors open and threw me the keys. "You know how to drive, don't you?"

I slid across the leather seat behind the wheel. This teenager's car might have been the nicest vehicle I'd ever sat in. I turned the key and "Good People" by Jack Johnson started coming out of her stereo, which was okay with me, because it was decent driving music, even if it was a little chick-ish. We drove the Lexus down the Eleventh Street hill to Pacific, then turned left and followed Pacific through downtown until Pacific turned into Schuster Parkway. We drove past Thea's Park, where the late-night skaters were jumping their boards down the big cement stairs. We went by the dark silhouettes of the grain terminals and the navy freighters that hugged the edge of Commencement Bay, past Northern Fish Co., and past the old fireboat I used to play around as a kid. We drove along the waterfront restaurants and parks to the far end of Ruston Way, where the ruins of a concrete pier made the abandoned beach look like an industrial Stonehenge. I turned off the ignition and stepped outside.

It was the last day of September, but the air was still warm. I threw the keys to Azura and jumped down to the beach. She followed. We climbed up the nearest pile of concrete and sat facing the rhythmic waves.

"You come here a lot?"

"I come here. Cars drive by, but no one seems to ever stop, so you get the beach all to yourself."

"You bring many girls down here?"

"Me? Nah. I'm more of a loner."

Azura laughed. "A what?"

I didn't repeat the word, since it didn't seem to work too well the first time.

Azura said, "That why I don't see you much at school?"

"What are you talking about? I go."

"Yeah, but I never see you at games. Or dances."

I broke off a bottlecap-sized piece of concrete and handed it to Azura. "You get right to it, don't you? That stuff is not really my thing."

"Why?"

"I don't know. Too many phonies, I guess."

She laughed. A rough laugh with that rough voice of hers. "You should come with me to Janine's party this Friday. We get all the phonies in one big room."

"Sounds awesome. You see that piling sticking out of the water? I'll give you fifty bucks if you can land your rock on it."

She stood up, trying to balance on the uneven surface. She put her left hand on my shoulder for support, leaning her legs against me. Her body was warm. She threw. Her bit of concrete hit the top of the piling and bounced into the water.

"Pay up."

"No, no, no. You only hit it. You didn't land on it." I stood next to her and threw. My rock missed the piling altogether.

She said, "I did better than you, though. That should be worth something."

"Like what?"

"Go to the party with me."

"No way."

That bottom lip came out again. "Then answer a question."

"Depends on the question."

"What are your parents like? Start with your mom."

"My mom? Man, you really are nosy."

"I am. Always have been. I hate small talk."

"But you like the phonies."

"Don't change the subject. Describe your mom to me."

"Can't we talk about something else? Ask me my favorite color."

"C'mon." She sat down like it was story time.

I sat down next to her, wondering what she was going to think of me, wishing I had a different story to tell. "All right. My mom's forty-nine percent free spirit and fifty-one percent cleaning lady."

"Be serious," said Azura, sticking out her bottom lip.

"That was serious, Miss Nosy. Those are the two sides of Mom's personality. At night, she cleans a handful of buildings for the same low-paying clients. And she does it without fail. She takes cleaning seriously. She's good at it. Too bad she isn't good at being a stockbroker or something that pays better. But she is good at cleaning. The rest of the time, she's way harder to pin down."

"Your mom sounds complicated. But you haven't really told me much, other than what she does. Tell me what she's like."

"I don't think so."

"Then how about your dad?"

"My who?"

"What's your dad do?"

"You ever notice how people always ask, 'What's your mom like?' But with Dads, they say, 'What's your dad do?' Doesn't matter, though. I don't have a dad. See, my mom is a cleaning lady. It's her job to keep everything immaculate. Even my conception." Azura just looked at me. "That was a joke," I said, "but I really don't have a dad."

I wondered why Azura was so interested in me. But I liked that she was. I found myself telling her what I'd rarely told anyone. Mom had been a teenage runaway from Spokane. She'd followed a cute college boy back to the University of Puget Sound in Tacoma when his Spokane summer job ended. That boy dumped Mom when school started, but not before he'd introduced her to a visiting philosophy professor. Apparently, the professor had used his philosophy to justify having sex with a minor. Eve got pregnant and the professor suddenly ended his visit and disappeared. And there I was, the sixteen-year-old kid of a single, thirty-three-year-old mother.

Now, once a month, a blue envelope arrived in the mail, never with a return address, usually with postmarks from one of three different cities: St. Louis; Pensacola, Florida; or Taos, New Mexico. The envelopes contained two hundred fifty dollars for rent, groceries, and basketball shoes, and a note.

"He sends you money and writes you notes, but you don't know who he is?"

"I have no idea who he is."

"You always lived in the same place?"

"No."

"Then how's he know where to send the money and the notes?"

"Don't know. And they're not regular notes. He just writes me questions. Riddles. When I was little, it was silly stuff like, 'How many animals did Moses take on the ark?'"

"How many?"

"Serious? Zero. Noah had the ark. Moses had the ten commandments."

"Wow. That's a really dumb joke. And kind of a cold note."

"I just got an envelope today. This time the note said, 'The world is dirty. So what's the point of staying clean?'"

"What's the answer?"

"You tell me."

"Sounds like a sweet guy. He'd get along great with my dad."

"Yeah, what about your dad? What'd he do to get that rich?"

"You want to know what he does, not what he's like?"

"No. I want to know what he *did.*"

"He just had to be born. But now he's an investment banker, whatever that means."

"It means money. That's enough."

"Maybe for you it is. Not for me."

"That's because you have so much."

She sighed, then broke off her own chunk of concrete and threw it into the water, this time aiming at nothing. "Now we're supposed to either get into a conversation about how I should be happy because I'm rich, or that money doesn't buy happiness, right?"

"Go for it."

"I like having money, if that's what you're asking. But— never mind."

"Never mind what?"

Azura broke off another chunk of concrete and threw it at the piling. She hit it square on the top, even from her seated position. "You should totally be paying me for my throwing skills."

"I can't afford to. I'm poor, remember?"

"Yeah. Let's talk about you. When you're not in school, what do you do?"

"I keep busy. I run errands for some of Mom's customers, like Nadel."

"Who?"

"Nadel of Nadel's House of Clocks. The guy fixing your old clock. Known him since I was a baby. Closest thing to a grandfather I have, I guess. I also cook a little bit at Shotgun Shack. You ever eaten there? No. I'm sure you haven't."

"You know how to cook?"

"I do. What can I get you? Fried chicken, perhaps?"

"Sounds kind of good right now. Are you going to be a chef someday?"

"Never thought about it. Just because I like it doesn't mean I want to do it for a job."

"But you do it for a job now."

"Yeah, but not much of one. I do it as much for fun as for money. I like cooking. The precision of it. I like being precise. And I spar, too."

"Spar?"

"I box. I work as a sparring partner for some of the boxers ChooChoo manages."

"You any good?"

"Compared to who? I'm not pro good, but I bet I could kick your butt. You wanna try it?" I punched her playfully on the chin, but she flinched and did not laugh. I wondered if she'd been hit before. I went in for a clinch and soon both my fists were behind her back, unclenching and pulling her close. She let me, for a second, then started play-punching me again. I laughed. That laugh felt good, but it felt temporary, too. What was I doing here with Azura? There was no way this rich girl had room for me in her life. Maybe for a day—a week, tops—but that was it. Then she'd get distracted by some shiny thing and leave me in her designer dust.

All this played through my brain, fighting against the soft scent of Azura's perfume. I pulled back. "Look, I got some stuff I gotta do. And you should probably get back home before Daddy calls the National Guard."

Azura frowned. "You've got *stuff*? Are you serious?"

"I should go."

"Then let me drive you."

"I can walk."

"Did something just happen that I missed?"

"I'm gonna go."

"We just met this morning, so why do I feel like we just broke up?"

I didn't answer, but I jumped down from the concrete pile and started walking east along the beach. I didn't turn around, because I didn't want to see the look on her lovely face—sad, pissed, happy, or heartbroken.

It was a long walk home. When I got there, it took me an hour to fall asleep.

Four

I awoke at three a.m. when a huge hand shook me gently by the shoulder. It took half a minute to wake-up enough to realize that ChooChoo was kneeling next to me, quietly whispering my name. His gentleness scared me.

"Y' gotta come downstairs," he said. His wet eyes caught the tiny bits of light in the room.

"What's wrong?"

"Your mom. She's—"

"She's what?"

"Dead. In her car. Out front."

I quickly pulled on some clothes and stumbled after ChooChoo through the dark gym. I could see colored lights flashing through the front windows. Blue meant police. Red meant ambulance.

Mom's jeep was parked crookedly along the curb. Her body was inside, slumped over the steering wheel. Three police cars and an ambulance had blocked off MLK. Bright bursts of light illuminated the scene. I slowly realized they were from a camera held by a cop taking pictures of the scene inside the car, his camera flash going off like lightning. I vaguely heard the crackly police radio voices, reciting numbers and words.

ChooChoo waved a weak hand and a plainclothes cop walked over to us, but I couldn't focus my eyes enough to see him clearly.

"I'm Detective Carlyle," the cop said. "You must be Seth." Carlyle spoke in a soft, lazy voice that he probably thought sounded comforting. "Sorry about your mom."

I barely heard him. I brushed past him to the driver's side of the Jeep. I pushed the photographer out of the way and pulled the door open. Then I stopped because I didn't know what to do next. Mom was still in her cleaning clothes—a men's white shirt and her old blue Dickies. I touched her hand. It was cold. I wanted to lift her head up from her awkward position, but I didn't want to see her face, now that the life was gone out of it. It wasn't my mom in that car. It was a ghoul and I didn't want to look at it anymore.

Detective Carlyle came over and made sure the photographer and police were done. They pulled Mom's body out of the car and onto a stretcher, covered it with a blanket, and slid it into the ambulance. I watched through the fingers I held over my eyes. Carlyle turned to me. "Did your mom have any health problems you know about?"

I barely managed a shrug.

"Did she use drugs?"

I didn't answer.

Carlyle rubbed his eyes and stared toward the closing ambulance doors. "Look, we don't need to talk about this anymore right now. I'll connect with you again tomorrow. But you shouldn't be alone tonight."

"I'm used to it."

"Not like this, you're not. I'm serious. You need to be with someone."

"Okay okay."

He turned to talk to ChooChoo and I noticed that tears were streaming down the big boxer's face. Not down mine. Crying didn't make sense to me. None of this did.

Mom's keys were still in the ignition. I jumped in the Jeep and slammed the door. Carlyle reached for the door handle, but I locked the car, then drove up on the sidewalk to get around the police cruisers. Carlyle's sleepy eyes followed me as I drove by him. A uniformed cop began running toward me, but Carlyle grabbed him by the arm and stopped him.

I had nowhere to go, but I wasn't looking for a destination. I just wanted to get away from that scene. I drove without direction, only occasionally registering a familiar landmark. Dock Street, sailboats, the Spar Tavern. I finally found myself on Carr Street and its beautiful Old Town homes with their water views. Mom had cleaned many of those homes over the years. Now she was dead and these rich people would never notice. And if they did, they wouldn't give a damn.

The world had tipped and it felt like I was sliding off the edge. I didn't know what to feel about Mom. Was I supposed to miss her or be mad at her? I was used to both situations. She was letting me down again. She was gone. She was dead and I didn't even know how she died. Was I heartbroken? Should I weep or curse? I pulled over to the nearest curb and turned off the engine. I leaned against the steering wheel, then pulled back as if it was electrified. The last thing to lean against that wheel was my mom's corpse. I jumped out of the car and slammed the door.

I found I'd parked in front of Azura's house. I'd needed someone and ended up at Azura. It was four a.m., but I walked up to the porch and knocked loudly on the door. I didn't care if I woke the whole house. An upstairs window lit up, then another. I heard a mile of footsteps before the front door opened.

The maid stood there, tying the belt of her robe. She said nothing, but I could see the confusion in the wrinkles of her forehead. *Why was this delivery boy here in the middle of the night?* Before she could say a word, she was pushed out of the way by a man who must have been Mr. Lear, Azura's father.

"What in God's name?" For someone who'd just rolled out of bed, his silver hair looked great. But red was showing through the tan of his face.

"I need to talk to Azura," I said.

"Not tonight, you don't. Who are you?"

"Could you just get her for me?"

"You need to leave before I call the police."

I thought about leaving. I thought about pushing my way inside. Then I heard more footsteps. The father turned and told someone to go back to bed. I heard Azura's sleepy voice asking what was going on.

"Nothing you need to worry about," Mr. Lear said. Azura saw me, then rushed past her father, grabbed my arm, and ran with me down to the Jeep, while Mr. Lear shouted behind us.

We drove back to Ruston Way. While I was driving, Azura kept asking me what was wrong, but I couldn't make the words come out. Finally, I stopped the car and told her what had happened. She said nothing, but her arms opened and I fell into them. I pretty well soaked her in tears.

"Seth?" Azura's voice finally broke our silence. "Do you want to tell me now?"

"Tell you what?"

"About her."

I was quiet for ten seconds then whispered, "Sometimes she was around. Sometimes she was gone all day. Sometimes she was sober. Sometimes she was so happy that she danced up and down the stairs to our apartment. And then sometimes she was so blue that she couldn't pull her head up from the couch cushions."

"Seth—"

"No. Listen. When I was in grade school, she'd show up for parent-teacher conferences halfway through or not at all. I got so sick of missing the conferences that I just started going on my own, from about fourth grade on. I'd come home angry from the conference and she'd wonder what I was so mad about. 'Oh honey,' she'd say, 'I was just living *in the moment.* You've got to learn to live *in the moment.*' I hated those words. 'Hey, Mom. How about, if every now and then, you tried living in one of my moments?' And then, just when I was about to commit to hating her forever, she'd take me on a weekend up to Seattle and we'd stay in a waterfront room at the Edgewater and eat piroshki and dim sum from Pike Place Market and see a movie on the big screen at the Cinerama and then go out to a fancy restaurant just for dessert and it would be magical and I would totally love her."

"That sounds nice."

"Sure. Then I'd hate her again when I found out that our weekend burnt through all the money for the entire month. 'Don't worry,' she'd say, with that wobbly-headed smile of hers. 'It'll all work out. You just need to learn to live in the *you-know-what.*'"

"What's a wobbly-headed smile?" asked Azura. "I don't know what that looks like."

"Sure you do. Old people have it. Or people with Parkinson's. Shaky people. Shaky old ladies who look at you and smile while their bobble heads are bobbling around."

"She had Parkinson's?"

"She had shaky."

"How old was she?"

"Young. Seventeen years older than me. So, uhh, thirty-three. She looked older than that most days. Her name is—was—Eve and she had thick black hair that was usually tied up in a knot on top of her head."

"That must be who you get your hair from. Yours kind of piles up on your head, too, Was she tall?"

"I'd say she's about five-six."

"Then your dad must be tall, because you're what—six one?"

"Five feet eleven-and-a-half. 'A fingernail shy of six feet,' Mom used to say."

"You look taller. How tall's your dad?"

I ignored the question. "Mom was pretty when she didn't look tired. Maybe even beautiful. The skin was always dark around her eyes—partly from being Italian, but partly from the way she lived. And her hands looked way older than the rest of her. Dry and cracked around the knuckles from all those years of dipping them in bleach water. And she was always doing this thing with her tooth."

"Explain."

"She had a chipped tooth right up front and she couldn't stop tracing it with her tongue. She hated that chipped tooth. 'It makes me look so cheap!' she'd say." I looked down at the floorboards, where my new Nike LeBrons were hidden in the shadows. "She just bought me these shoes today. Didn't figure them for a damned going-away present."

We fell into silence again, which was fine by me.

Five

I never went back to sleep that night. Azura wrote her phone number on the palm of my hand. I brought Azura to her house in time for school, then sat in Mom's Jeep in front of the boxing gym, listening to music, wishing a song would comfort me. None did. At ten a.m., I walked into ChooChoo's office either to see how he was doing or to see how I was doing through his eyes. The walls of his office were lined in old boxing posters and photographs. Some of the posters listed him in the main events at big matches, including one at Caesar's Palace in Las Vegas and another at Madison Square Garden in New York City.

A few years ago, Mom had told me that ChooChoo used to box heavyweight and that'd he'd been a serious contender for the championship belt.

"What happened?" I'd asked Mom.

"His temper. He boxed with rage. In one of his last bouts, he beat the other guy so badly that the man couldn't ever make a decent sentence again. Just mumbled. ChooChoo had only one match after that. In that next one, he killed a man outright. Had him up against the ropes and just kept beating him. His own trainers had to pull him off. ChooChoo wasn't charged with a crime, but he was fined fifty thousand dollars and suspended for two years. When his suspension ended, he couldn't get a fight. No one wanted to get into the ring with him. Finally, he quit trying and opened this gym."

I looked at that Madison Square Garden poster. It had been printed with a bright yellow background—but the yellow had faded in spots. A stack of big red letters said, "15 ROUNDS FOR THE HEAVYWEIGHT CHAMPIONSHIP OF THE WORLD LEON LAMONT UNDEFEATED HEAVYWEIGHT CHAMPION VS. CHOOCHOO BALDWIN UNDEFEATED KO KING." On either side of the words were black-and-white images of the two boxers. A younger, thinner ChooChoo had his gloves up and a mean, steady look in his eyes. His black skin contrasted with his white shorts and shoes.

ChooChoo had grown fat since then, but still looked powerful enough to win in the ring. Right now, he was sitting at his desk, ignoring a stack of papers. The desk also held a cheaply framed photograph of ChooChoo and my mom. I'd seen it hundreds of times, but I picked it up. The picture was about ten years old. Their heads were leaning in toward each other. Both smiled and looked worry-free. Happy was probably the right word for it.

ChooChoo's attention seemed to be on a Styrofoam cup of coffee. Without looking up, he said, "Y' mom use t' pay me three hundred a month, an' she was my girlfrien'. You don't have t' pay that much, but ya gotta pay somp'n. Can ya do two hundred?"

"I think so."

"Maybe you c'n spar some, too."

"Sure. I would anyway."

He took a sip from his cup and shuddered. "Wors' coffee inna world. Dam' that Manny."

"Take another hundred bucks off the rent and I could take care of the coffee, too."

"You know how t' make coffee?"

"I'll learn. I guarantee it will be better than that stuff."

"Deal. Ya make coffee. Ya spar. An' one hundred a month." He looked up at me. "You okay?"

"Not really."

"Me neither."

He stared at me a few seconds and then said, "Seth, got one other condition. Ya can't go it alone. Ya got t' get y'self a fam'ly."

"A what?"

"A fam'ly. Ya c'n stay here 'f you get y'self one."

"What, like you want me to get adopted?"

"Naw. Not talkin' 'bout no legal fam'ly. Talkin' bout real fam'ly. People ya c'n count on. People who have t' count on you. People who, 'f you drive 'em crazy or ev'n 'f you go crazy'll stick by you 'n bail you outta whatever place you th'own into."

"I take it you mean more than just you."

"Y' don' wanna hafta depen' on me, son."

After a few seconds, I said, "I'm not sure I can do that, Chooch. Family and me don't really go together. My dad is a deadbeat and my mom is just dead. And even when she was alive, she was pretty much a dud."

ChooChoo jumped up from his seat and slapped me across the face, sending me sprawling toward a far wall. "Don' talk 'bout yer mom that way, boy," ChooChoo said, looking at me from behind his desk. "She did for you 'n ways you'll never know."

I stood up and walked out, with my hand to my face. I was tired of hurting.

I went upstairs and laid on the couch, trying to sleep for a few hours. When I got up, it was mid-afternoon, which meant it would be a slow time at Guinevere's, a coffee shop six blocks down the hill. I walked, hoping I wouldn't see anyone I knew along the way.

My favorite barista at Guinevere's was Nikki, a girl I'd had a crush on since fifth grade. Nikki was a year older than me and a grade above me. Her blond hair was cut spiky and short off her elfin ears. Her eyes were a blue so pale that she might have been birthed by wolves. She embellished the coveted parts of her body in magic marker scribbles and ever-changing henna tattoos. Today, a brown skull with snakes coming out of the eye sockets covered the skin at the unbuttoned collar of her shirt.

The first time I ever went into Guinevere's was the day after it opened. I'd walked in suspiciously, curious to see if a decent coffee shop was a possibility within walking distance of my home. I hadn't expected to be greeted by Nikki, but that was all it took for Guinevere's to instantly become one of my favorite places. I'd taken a deep breath and ordered a double shot of espresso.

"Sure you don't want a hot chocolate, studly?" Nikki had asked, looking at me from underneath her bangs. "Maybe with some sprinkles?"

"I don't like sweet stuff."

"Guess I'll have to take your word for that." Nikki took my money, smiled slightly, and put my change into her tip jar without asking. She ground the beans, tamped them firm, and shot steam through them until the brown-black espresso dripped into a tiny white cup. She handed the cup to me and watched me drink the whole thing. She nodded at me and said, "You have a natural taste for the bitter."

This time, when I walked into her shop, a couple of slackers sat nursing cappuccinos at tables while they hunched over their laptops. Otherwise, the café was empty. The place was tiny, with only enough seats for about a dozen narrow-bodied customers. The walls were a half-inch-thick in rock posters of local bands with names like Goldfinch, Pablo Trucker, Motopony, and Youth Rescue Mission. "White Winter Hymnal" by Fleet Foxes was playing on her stereo. The counter Nikki stood behind was red Formica and chrome, like a diner from the 1950s. "'Sup, studly? How come you weren't at school today?"

"I need you to show me how to make coffee."

"Can't. Trade secret. If I told you, I'd have to—"

"—kill me? Doesn't sound so bad right now."

"What's wrong with you?"

"Nothing I want to talk about."

Nikki shrugged. She was the rare person who knew when to stop asking questions. I explained to her matter-of-factly how ChooChoo had agreed to give me a discount on rent if I took care of the coffee at his gym.

"Then I guess it better be good coffee. Come on back here." I walked around the red-and-chrome counter. Nikki filled a white enamel teapot with water and set it on a gas burner. "Whatcha got to brew in?" I started describing ChooChoo's old, stained coffeemaker until Nikki cut me off. "If you promise not to tell my boss, I can cut you a deal on some of Guinevere's old gear—a grinder, a French press, and, unless Chooch is gonna drink all the coffee in one sitting, a thermos. And you're gonna need beans. I might be able to hook you up with the beans for free, if you're nicer to me than you're being today."

When she said that, I almost started bawling on the spot. I don't know why.

The teapot was whistling by now, so Nikki turned off the gas. The flame disappeared with a soft *whup*. Nikki picked up a small metal scoop and shook it at me. "Now pay attention. Good coffee is all about the details. First of all, only grind as many beans as you're gonna make right away."

She poured dark brown beans into the top of the grinder and flipped a switch for a few seconds, then turned the grinder off. "See that? Coarse ground. Not espresso ground. You don't want to grind them too fine or ChooChoo will be drinking a cup of sludge. Then you scoop out one scoop per cup. If you're making six cups, how many scoops you gonna use?"

"Six."

"Genius. If you lose the scoop, one rounded tablespoon. But don't skimp. Scoop it in quick, because coffee starts going stale the minute it's ground."

Nikki picked up the teapot. "Get your water boiling then take it off the heat before you start grinding. By the time your grinding is done, your water will be just about the perfect temperature. And make sure your French press is one hundred percent clean. If I find out you used a dirty press, I'll ban you from this shop." Nikki poured a few inches of steaming water into the glass cylinder. "Cover the grounds. Make sure you get them all the way wet, but don't fill the press. The beans will gas off a bit." Brown foam formed on the surface of the liquid as she spoke. "Then slowly pour in the rest of your water. Use a butter knife or the handle of a wooden spoon and give the coffee a quick stir to make sure you get all the flavor out of the grounds. Just a few stirs. Then put on the lid. Now we've got four minutes for you to tell me what the hell is going on."

I told her. She stared at the ceiling. When I was done, Nikki silently guided me back to the waiting coffee. She placed my hand on the plunger of the French press and pushed it down slowly. She poured the dark liquid into a white ceramic cup, then handed it to me, touching my hand as she did so. She took my hand in hers and held it as I sipped. The coffee was hot and bitter.

Six

I decided to go back home and call the police to see what I was supposed to do about Mom's body. I went upstairs and called the number on Detective Carlyle's card. He didn't answer. I left a message.

I was tired, so I lay down on Mom's daybed and tried to sleep. I failed for a good hour, but finally drifted off. I woke up when the phone rang at five o'clock. It was an automated message from Heath High School. The computerized voice let me know that Seth Anomundy had missed all his classes with an unexcused absence and that if I had any questions I should call the school office.

I'd missed school today, but what was I supposed to do tomorrow? Just go back like nothing had happened? The phone rang again and interrupted my thoughts. It was Carlyle, asking if he could come over and talk to me. I said yes and hung up.

While I was waiting, I decided to brew a batch of coffee for ChooChoo and walked down to the car to retrieve the equipment Nikki had given me. I went outside and reached my hand in my pocket for the keys.

Right then, a cobalt blue Volvo wagon pulled up behind me, almost hitting me with its front bumper. This wagon had seventeen-inch rims, custom paint, and "Over" by Drake rattling its tinted windows. I'd always hated that song. Four high school boys climbed out. I knew all of them, but not in a good way. Two with crew cuts wore loose practice football jerseys that couldn't hide their round, muscular shoulders. They were twin brothers, actually, named Zach and Cody. I'd been through a few years of phys ed. classes with them, amazed at their ability to climb ropes, snap towels, and stand around naked without shame. The third kid was a thick, red-haired brute who was at least six-three and had to weigh two-fifty. His name was Carl, but everyone called him Big Red. He was on Heath's football team, too. A fullback. Not a great open-field runner, but he could always be counted on for three yards right up the middle. The fourth, Erik Jorgenson—there was no other word for him but gorgeous. If our high school was a kingdom then Erik was the haughty prince. He seemed to letter in every sport and was the kid who always seemed to get his name mentioned at all-school assemblies. Whenever it happened, sixteen hundred kids would chant, Jor-gee, Jor-gee, Jor-gee. I'd even chanted along a few times. His dad was a surgeon and Erik was fit, tan, blond, and carrying a baseball bat.

Gorgeous Erik led all four boys over to me and said, "What's up, Seth? You *trying* to make your life difficult?"

I was staring at that bat, wondering what answer would help me avoid adding to Erik's batting average.

He said, "You deaf? I asked you a question."

"Sorry, I was too busy focusing on that baseball bat to hear what you said. I like how you went for wood instead of aluminum. Old school."

"All right, smartass, how about if we skip the small talk and we just beat the crap out of you?"

"For what?"

"For hanging around Azura."

"Serious? You and her still going out? Because she didn't mention you."

Gorgeous Erik pulled the bat back and swung. He missed me on purpose. Man, he had a beautiful swing. Stepped into it with his right foot with whole-body follow-through that reminded me of young Ichiro Suzuki. Erik had put in some time at the plate. I wondered how he was at fielding ground balls until Big Red snuck up on my left and hit me in the stomach. I doubled over. I hadn't seen that one coming. "Your mouth is just making this worse, jackass" said Red. "Just shut up and keep away from her."

I stood back up faster than Red expected me to. All my sparring in ChooChoo's ring had given me pretty tough abs. I popped Red in his own stomach. His hands came down to block another blow, just like I knew they would, and I landed a one-two combination on his chin, knocking him back into his friends. If they hadn't caught him, he'd have been sitting on his butt. These North End boys never really knew how to fight. They lacked my experience—both in the ring and on the street. But that wooden bat and their superior numbers still made me nervous.

Erik took another swing with the bat and almost hit me. He was trying this time and I could feel the wind. Zach and Cody, the two football players, were circling around behind. I didn't know where to give my attention.

"Hey Erik, did you even ask Azura what she thought about this?"

"None of your damn business."

"It's my business if you come beating on me about it. Why don't you send your friends home, put down the wussy bat and face me like a man?" I was hoping my stupid courage would catch them off guard.

"Nice try," Erik said. He was smarter than I expected. Zach and Cody rushed me and grabbed my arms before I could get away. They were strong as young gorillas. I'd have bruises on my biceps by the time they let go. Now that I couldn't fight back, Big Red took another swing at my stomach. I had to give the boy some credit. He hit me like a sledgehammer this time. His hit lifted my feet off the ground.

Then Gorgeous Erik took his turn. He used the bat like a battering ram and assaulted my gut. He took a swing at my face, but I pulled back enough so he only grazed the whiskers of my chin. He went after my stomach again. It hurt.

A police siren sounded. A cop car pulled up to check out the commotion, like they tend to do in my neighborhood. Despite my pain, the flashing blue lights brought my mind back to the night before. Erik dropped the bat. His friends let go of me and adjusted their postures. I collapsed to the ground.

From where I lay on the sidewalk, I saw the passenger door of the police car open and a pair of black boots step out. I heard the driver's side door open and close. Another set of boots joined the first. Leather-clad hands reached down and pulled me to my feet. "What's going on, fellas?" said the cop from the driver's side.

"Nothing, officer," said Erik. "Just hanging out."

I'd seen the cop driving around our streets before, but I'd never talked to him. He looked at the four strangers. "You boys aren't from this neighborhood, are you?"

"No sir."

"You should be careful around here." He looked at me and frowned. "You there. You giving these boys any trouble?" I frowned back. The cop didn't like that. "What's your name again?" I told him. "Spell it." I spelled it. S-E-T-H. A-N-O-M-U-N-D-Y. "Chambers, run a record check on this kid." Chambers, the other cop, climbed into the patrol car and spoke on the radio for a few minutes. He stuck his head out and said, "C'mere for a second, Dix." Dix the driver walked over and the two spoke in low tones. When he was done, Dix approached me and said, "Sounds like you had a pretty solid gathering of police here just last night. And it sounds like you got enough trouble already without hassling these boys. Seems like a strange time for you to be stirring things up. So we'll give you a break this time. Take this as a gift—and as a warning—and stay out of trouble." Without saying a word to the four beautiful jocks, Dix climbed into the car and he and Chambers drove away.

"You see how it is now, son?" asked Erik, once the car was out of sight. "You see who runs the show?" His voice was fast and high. I expected him to start high-fiving his friends. He picked up the bat and poked me in the chest. "Stay away from Azura." They left and I sat back down on the sidewalk.

There was no way Azura sent those guys. And we hadn't seen anyone when we were together. That meant her father, Mr. Lear, had decided to sic them on me. He probably rounded them up at the tennis club and offered them future internships at his investment firm. They were what Azura's North End world had always looked like to me—well-funded, college-bound, and vicious.

After five minutes of sucking wind on the sidewalk, I gathered Nikki's brewing equipment from Mom's Jeep and headed back inside my apartment. My cell phone rang. Caller ID said it was the Tacoma Police Department. I wasn't much in the mood, but I answered. Detective Carlyle's voice came on, letting me know he was outside. I asked him to come in.

In case he wanted to start punching me, I'd rather it happened inside ChooChoo's building.

Carlyle came in the apartment and sat on our old couch, looking surprisingly at home. His eyes were mostly closed and his clothes were wrinkled. I'd guess Carlyle was five-eight and probably weighed two-ten. He had a square head and a square body, with a torso about as deep as it was wide. His half-closed eyes made him look both sad and sleepy.

"You called me with some questions. And I've got some news. You want me to go first?"

"I guess." I pulled a chair from the kitchen table and straddled it backwards, the chair back like a shield between Carlyle and me.

"Final autopsy report is not in yet." Carlyle rubbed his palms into his eyes. "But there were signs of death by a toxic substance."

"Toxic? You mean poison?"

Carlyle stared at me. "Something like that."

"So, like suicide?"

Carlyle shrugged. "Could be accidental, suicide, or I suppose even homicide."

"Homicide? Like *murder* homicide?"

"Means we'll have to hold on to your mom's body for a few more days."

"And then what? You give it back to me?"

"For funeral purposes. Yes."

"A funeral? I'm probably supposed to figure that out somehow, huh?"

"Probably. Find someone to help you, Seth. You must have people in your life you can turn to. Family."

"Yeah. I must have."

Carlyle asked me some questions about Mom's cleaning customers. I told him about the church, Shotgun Shack, Nadel, and the driving school. He said he'd start with those people, but asked if there was anyone else she might have seen on her last day alive. The only other people I could think of were ChooChoo and me. I told him so.

I didn't tell him about Mom's final conversation with me—how she'd got in a shouting match with Miss Irene and how it upset her enough for her to buy me an expensive pair of shoes. I didn't tell him because I didn't want to think Miss Irene was anything other than innocent.

Seven

That night, I lay on Mom's daybed and texted Azura. She responded immediately, asking how my day was. *Interesting,* I texted.

Interesting how?

Police told me Mom might have been murdered.

Serious?

Serious. Poisoned.

By who?

They don't know. Maybe it was suicide, but I don't think so.

I did something you might not like.

What? I texted.

I told one of the school counselors about your mom.

Which one.

Ms. Edelson. She said she'd call you.

Why'd you tell her?

Because I think you needed me to. Are you mad?

Not about that.

About what?

A group of your friends visited me.

Friends? Who?

Erik, Big Red, and the twins.

Oh. replied Azura.

Yes. Oh.

What'd they do?

Told me to stay away from you, then beat me with a baseball bat.

You're kidding.

Wish I was.

I'm gonna call Erik.

Not necessary.

I'm gonna anyway. Then I'm coming over.

Maybe that's not a good idea. Don't think my stomach could stand another beating.

There was a long pause before Azura texted back. *You want me to stay away?*

I replied immediately. *I want you to come over.*

She knocked on my door fifteen minutes later. I still didn't invite her in. We stood on the walkway outside my door as she checked me for bruises and broken bones. It wasn't unpleasant. When the exam ended, I asked where she wanted to go. She suggested coffee. I suggested Guinevere's.

The coffee shop was busy—the little tables overcrowded with the tattooed, the pierced, and the voluntarily outcast. The stereo was playing some clickity-clack song by the Books just loud enough to blend in with the crowd noise. A man with a shaved head, nose ring, and hugely gauged earlobes grinned widely at us from a table near the counter. Azura grabbed my arm tightly, right on the same spot the twins had bruised me earlier.

Nikki appeared from behind the steaming espresso machine. I introduced her to Azura and Nikki said hi with raised eyebrows, looking at me sideways as she said it.

"What?" I said, but Nikki just asked what we wanted. I ordered two cappuccinos and a black currant scone. Azura tried to pay, but I pushed her money away. "I got it."

"I can pay for myself, you know."

"I'm sure you can."

"I can order for myself, too. I'm a big girl. How do you know what I want?"

"Trust me," I said. "This is the best cappuccino in town."

We found a table in the corner. Nikki brought our coffee and scones to us, instead of calling from the counter.

"You have table service now?" I asked.

"Just for you, studly." She sat down next to me, pushing me half off my wooden chair. "Mind if I take my break here for a few minutes?" Azura smiled, but only with her mouth. Nikki said, "You go to Heath, right?"

"I do," said Azura.

"Thought I'd seen you before. How'd you two meet? At school?"

"At my house, actually."

"Really? Seth makes house calls?"

"About as often as you wait on tables," I said quietly.

Nikki nodded to Azura. "You haven't tried your coffee."

Azura took a sip of her cappuccino. She grimaced.

"You don't like it?" Nikki asked.

"I usually get something more, umm, syrupy."

"I bet you do," said Nikki.

"Be nice, Nikki," I said.

She turned on me. "I'm being nice. This is what me being nice looks like. But I'm confused. Your mom just died. And yet, you're feeling good enough to take this girl out on a date?"

I wanted to explain to Nikki that it wasn't a date. Not really. But I didn't want to say the words out loud. I said nothing. Nikki sat in the silence for a few seconds, then left without a word.

"Nice girl," said Azura.

"She *is* a nice girl."

"That's what I said."

"It's not what you say. It's how you say it."

"Tell that to your friend. The nice girl. The pit bull."

"Pit bull? That's the dog of my people. You have a dog?"

"I do."

"What kind? Wait. Don't tell me. Something mixed with a poodle."

Azura glared at me, then took a big gulp of her cappuccino. Her lips smiled while her eyes continued to glare. "You think my life is all lovely?"

"Not all lovely, but—"

"But what? You think I have it so much better than you. You've met my dad. I guarantee he's the one who sent those boys after you. It doesn't even surprise me."

"Okay, so maybe we've both got it rough. You've got a dad who beats up boys who like you and I've got a murdered mom."

Azura reached across the table and touched the back of my hand with the tips of her fingers. Her hand stayed there. So did mine. "Is that what it is?"

"What?"

"I've been trying to figure out what I like about you."

"Gee, thanks."

"Shut up. You're good-looking, in your own rough way. You know it. But there's—something. I don't know."

"Maybe I'm just not a phony like all your other friends."

"Maybe." She dipped her finger in her cappuccino foam, then looked at it. "You'd think at least the foamy part would be sweet. So what are you going to do?" she asked.

"I don't know. It freaks me out, thinking of Mom being murdered, but it kind of relieves me, in a weird sort of way. If she was poisoned, that means she didn't OD. It means she wasn't to blame this time. She was a victim. That means I can be mad at someone else."

Azura took another sip of her cappuccino. No grimace. "Once you know it's going to be bitter, it's not so bad. Do the police have any leads?"

"Not that they told me." I broke off a piece of scone and held it up to Azura. Her lips stayed closed. "You'll like this."

"That's what you said about the coffee."

"And you like it. I know you do. Or you will." I offered the scone again. Her lips parted and I placed the bit of bread into her mouth. Azura chewed and smiled at the same time.

"Can I ask you a question?" she said, after she swallowed. "Is this a date?"

"It could be. Could it be?"

"It could be. After all, you said you like me."

"Uhh…"

"You said my dad beats up boys who like me. You got beat up. So…"

"I wasn't thinking about what I was saying."

Azura's eyes grew wide. She smiled, then picked up the scone and bit off a big piece. She chewed, then took another sip of coffee.

"I called Erik before I came over."

"Yeah? What'd he have to say?"

"I told him your mom died yesterday. I think it kind of freaked him out."

"Like that should matter. He's a jerk."

"He's not that bad."

"They travel in packs—guys like him who aren't that bad." She sipped her coffee, then stood up from the table.

"Where you going?" I asked.

"I need some sugar."

We sat and talked and sat without talking for two more hours. I told Azura she needed to get home before her dad sent out another country-club search party. I said good-bye to Nikki, but she just glared at me. Azura and I drove back to the gym and parked. I walked her to her car. It was a beautiful car. She was a beautiful girl. Both looked out of place in my neighborhood. Strike that. My neighborhood had beautiful girls, too. But they had the grit to stick it out. I doubted the same would be true of Azura. She would be gone soon. She was too fragile to stay around.

Instead of opening the car door, she leaned against it, then turned toward me. "I know what you're thinking," she said.

"You do?"

"Yes. You're thinking that I'm beautiful."

"Serious?"

"Yup. And you're wondering if you should kiss me."

"You think everyone wants to kiss you all the time?"

"Don't know about everyone. But I think you want to. And you're wondering if I'd let you. I would. And you're wondering if it would be a good idea. It would. And you're wondering—"

"I'm wondering when you're gonna shut up." I kissed her.

The street in front of the gym was empty and dark in a way that only a city street can be dark. Headlights, sign lights and stoplights were still blazing. The wet black streets in front of the gym picked up all that glare and all that color and bounced it up and into Azura's eyes.

"What am I thinking now?" I asked.

"Nothing," she said, kissing me back. "Not one little thing."

Eight

My alarm clock woke me up the next morning in time to get ready for school. I decided not to go. But I was still downstairs thirty minutes before ChooChoo usually arrived at the gym. I boiled water, ground beans, and brewed enough French-press coffee to fill the big thermos pot right to the top. I went back upstairs to shower and dress, planning to head over to Shotgun Shack and see Miss Irene.

When I went back downstairs, ChooChoo, Manny, and two other trainers were gathered around the coffee pot, swapping stories and refilling cups. "Hey, kid," yelled Manny. "You might of done Chooch a disservice, making coffee this good. No one's gonna want to get in the ring if it means leaving this pot."

They all laughed. ChooChoo said, "Ya done fine. Prob'ly get mo' coffee cust'mers than boxing cust'mers. You goin' t' school t'day?" I shook my head no. ChooChoo nodded.

I joined them for a cup. I needed their kind words—even if they were just about my brewing skills. And props to Nikki and me: it was damn good coffee.

I drove Mom's jeep over to Shotgun Shack and went inside, but Miss Irene wasn't there. Checker Cab was doing the cooking *and* the table waiting and he wasn't happy about it. I asked after Miss Irene and Checker snapped at me, "I don't know where that old woman is. Phone rang yesterday afternoon and after she hung up, she just cleared out without saying a thing. So I closed the place down last night all by myself, then still had to clean up, 'cause of your mom not being around anymore. Sorry about that, by the way. Then I opened again this morning because I couldn't get ahold of Miss Irene. She's disappeared."

Checker Cab glared at the dishes stacked up on tables all around the dining room. "Looks like I'll be closing again tonight. That means overtime. That means getting paid. But who's gonna sign my check?"

Checker begged me to stick around and help out with the lunch rush. He said he'd pay me right out of the till for my time and he'd split his tips with me. I knew Checker would rip me off somehow, but I agreed and moved into my old spot in the kitchen. For the next three hours, I was elbow-deep in catfish, hush puppies, and collard greens. I'd never run the kitchen by myself and it showed. I was behind all through lunch and the diners were barking at Checker, which made him bark at me. But the rush finally ended and I hadn't thought about my mom the whole time. Checker gave me thirty bucks for my three hours, then fudged around in the cash register, finally giving me another twenty dollars, which he claimed was half his share of tips. I knew he undercut me by at least another twenty, but I expected it from Checker. I didn't like him any less for it. I didn't like him much to begin with.

I headed back home, wondering where Miss Eye had disappeared to and wondering how her disappearance connected to Mom's death. Hopefully not at all. Right when I was thinking about it, my cell phone rang. It was Carlyle, asking if I had a few minutes to come down to the station.

I didn't like cops. In my neighborhood, cops only came to bring bad news or bad times. Carlyle seemed like a decent guy, but I didn't much want to go down to a whole station full of police.

But I went. I parked out front, made sure I put enough change in the meter to avoid a ticket, and walked inside. As I was going through the front doors, Dix and Chambers, the cops who'd rescued Erik Jorgenson and his friends from me, were walking out.

"Here comes trouble," Dix said, elbowing Chambers and nodding at me. I tried to walk by, but Dix grabbed me by the wrist. "Slow down there, cowboy. You just can't get enough of Tacoma's Finest these days, can you?"

"I'm here to see Carlyle."

"Ahh. About your mommy. Sad story." His tone dropped in volume, to a level he probably thought was fatherly. "Look kid, you caught a tough break. No doubt. You should forget about it and move on. Because that's what we're gonna do. We're gonna forget about it. No one here has time to try to find the killer of a woman like your mom. She doesn't register high on the priority list, if you understand."

"I understand *you*, if that's what you mean."

"Hey, nothing personal, kid. Just the way things are."

I yanked my arm free and walked inside. I could hear my heart beating in my head. I tried to sound calm when I gave my name to a policewoman at a desk. But I wasn't calm. I wanted to hit something. I wanted to break my hand on a wall of sheetrock.

Carlyle came out to meet me within a minute. He studied my face for a second and said, "Something happen I need to know about?"

"Just a couple of your jackass buddies."

"Dix and Chambers?"

"You must be so proud to work with them."

"Yeah, they mentioned that they ran into you yesterday. They're jerks. Try to ignore them and c'mon back to my desk for a minute. Can I get you a cup of coffee?"

"No thanks. I'm a bit of a coffee snob."

"Then stay away from this stuff." He led me to a cubicle in a sea of cubicles, all in matching gray fabric. I sat in a stained, gray chair next to his pressboard desk. It sure didn't look like the cop shows on TV. Here the cops mostly just looked tired—almost as tired as the furniture. Everything in the building seemed underfunded and overworked.

"We've got some more information about your mom. I'm not sure if you'll think it's good news or not. She tested positive for cyanide. She was poisoned, all right."

"So she was murdered?"

"Can't tell."

"What can you tell?"

Carlyle sighed. He opened a folder on his desk and pulled out a blue piece of paper. He read:

"'Samples, such as peripheral blood, stomach contents, bile fluid, urine, and mouth swabs, were prepared using visible spectrophotometric method. The cyanide contents in samples, included stomach content—two hundred and sixty parts per million bile fluid—two hundred seventy-two parts per million, blood—two hundred fifty-six parts per million, and mouth swab—two hundred sixty-five parts per million. Conclusion: The cause of death was acute myocardial infarction following acute poisoning from ingestion of cyanide."

"Which means what?"

"Which means just what I said. She was poisoned. We can't rule out suicide yet, but I'm telling you that homicide seems likely. Based on time of death, my guess is that she was poisoned, then driven back to the gym by her killer who moved her into the driver's seat." He watched my face for a reaction. I tried not to have one. "Seth, we've followed up with the businesses your mom did cleaning for. And we found something interesting. One of her clients has run away. Disappeared. Irene Dunlop. She owns a restaurant called Shotgun Shack."

"I know who she is, and she—"

"Hold on. According to an employee, she's been having a number of heated arguments with your mom. And just yesterday, I talked to Irene on the phone, but only for about thirty seconds. She cut the conversation short. She definitely did not want to talk to me. According to her employee, she left the restaurant right after that and no one's seen her since."

Carlyle thought I'd be happy that he had a suspect. But I told him he was crazy. Sure, Miss Irene and Mom argued, but I explained how there was no way that she would ever hurt my mother.

"Then why did she run away?"

"How would I know? Are you checking out anybody else?"

"Like I said, we checked everybody. We don't *have* any other leads. And we don't have a lot of resources to spare on a case like this, Seth."

"*A case like this.* Yeah, that's what Dix told me."

Carlyle sighed. "Look. I'll do what I can, but it's not gonna be much. Especially when this Dunlop woman looks like such a clear suspect."

"It wasn't her," I said. "It can't be. I'll prove it to you if I have to."

"How?"

"I have no idea."

"You need to keep out of it."

"I need to know what really happened."

Carlyle shook his head as he looked at me through his half-opened eyes. "Seth, if someone truly murdered your mom, that someone is obviously dangerous. A smart kid like you will leave the matter to the police. You are a smart kid, aren't you?"

Nine

I went back home. It was almost five o'clock, which was usually a busy time for ChooChoo, but the gym was nearly empty. He was pushing a broom in his graceful way, weaving it around a heavy bag hanging from the ceiling. That big man couldn't take a step without looking like an athlete. He smiled up at me with watery eyes.

"Thinkin' 'bout y' mom jus' now."

"Me, too." I told him what Carlyle had said. While he listened, his hands clenched the broom handle so tight I thought he'd snap it in two. He asked me what I was going to do. I said that I wanted to help figure out who might have killed Mom, but I had no idea where to start.

ChooChoo set down the broom and threw me a set of gloves and a sparring helmet. "I got no idea, either. But climb into th' ring wimmee. Little sparring might knock sump'n loose 'n y' brain."

I never liked sparring with ChooChoo, because he didn't know how to go easy. He outweighed me by at least a hundred pounds and he pulled his punches, but they still hurt in a way that felt like permanent damage. It cleared my head like nothing else could. In the ring with ChooChoo, all my focus went toward hitting and not getting hit. When ChooChoo was swinging, I couldn't worry about girls, money, or Mom. If I lost my focus for a second, my head would be ringing and I'd be blinking at the ceiling.

Like always, I tried to use my speed as a defense. Like always, ChooChoo was faster than I expected. He kept up with me and cut off my angles until he had me against the ropes. I'd try to duck under his jabs and get into open space, but he'd dance to the side and be in front of me again.

Our bout ended like it always ended, with ChooChoo helping me to my feet after knocking me down.

"Ya think of anything?" he asked. He still had his mouth guard in, but sounded the same as when it was out.

"Yeah, I think you might have dislocated my jaw."

He laughed. It was good to hear.

"Chooch, I don't know where I'd even start on something like this."

"Then ya start wit' the easy stuff. Ya start wit' whachoo know an' ya take it from there."

My cell phone rang while I was walking up the stairs to the apartment. It was the high school computer voice again, reminding me that Seth Anomundy had missed another day of school. "Thanks for caring," I said, as I hung up.

I was tired. I took a quick shower and went around the corner to the Vietnamese restaurant, Pho Bac, and brought back a couple of Styrofoam to-go containers of their noodle soup. ChooChoo and I crushed fresh basil and slices of lime into the broth. We ate in silence. Afterwards, I went upstairs and went to sleep.

I woke up the next morning, decided to avoid school again, did my coffee duty, and headed back to Shotgun Shack to see what more I could learn about Miss Irene's disappearance.

After that, my plan was to start retracing Mom's steps of her last night, keeping in mind ChooChoo's direction to focus on the easy stuff. If there was any.

It was ten a.m. when I parked in front of the restaurant. Not a single customer was inside—not even Stanley Chang. I wondered if he'd stopped coming around once Miss Irene disappeared. Checker Cab was wiping down tables after the breakfast crowd and getting the kitchen ready for lunch. He wasn't interested in talking to me.

"What is it you want, exactly?" he said, while he did a quick and crummy job sweeping beneath the tables.

"I'm trying to figure out who might have killed my mom."

"Killed? Is that what you think happened?"

"The police say she was murdered. She was poisoned. With cyanide. Then her body was probably driven home and parked in front of the gym."

Checker Cab stopped sweeping for a minute and leaned his big belly against the broom. "Murdered. Hard to believe." He paused. "Is there a reward?"

"Reward? For what?"

"You know, for information leading to the whereabouts and all that?"

"I don't think the cops are offering anything."

"How about you?"

"Me?"

"Yeah, any reward from your end?"

"You're kind of a jerk, you know that?"

"I'm a businessman. That's all."

"Okay, Checker. If you got some information that leads to the case getting solved, I'll pay you."

"How much?"

I had no idea what a lot of money was for someone like Checker Cab. "A hundred dollars?"

"Seth, I won't get out of bed for less than two hundred."

"Okay. Two hundred dollars."

"For two hundred, I'll keep an eye peeled. For three hundred, I'll keep both eyes peeled, washed, and ready for the pot."

I thought about the small amount of cash in the Gold'n Soft tub. Three hundred dollars would hurt, but I was willing to pay if it helped me find Mom's killer. "Okay. Three hundred. But the way they say it on TV is that you only get paid if your info actually helps solve the case. Same deal here."

"Same deal is fine by me." He walked the broom toward the kitchen, leaving half the dining room unswept.

I asked Checker if he could tell me anything more about where Miss Irene might have gone. He yelled that if he knew where she was, he would have dragged her back to the restaurant. I asked if he was here when Miss Irene and Mom fought on that last night.

"I was here. But I probably would have heard them even if I was home. Them women can turn up the volume. Good lord. Hey, you wanna work the lunch shift again today? I can't keep doing this on my own."

"Can't today, Checker. I got some investigating to do."

I left, thinking about Miss Irene. She ran away the day after Mom died. There had to be a connection. But I still couldn't imagine that Miss Irene could have poisoned Mom.

If Miss Irene wasn't guilty, why did she leave? And where did she go?

I decided to work my way through Mom's customers. I left the Jeep in front of Shotgun Shack and walked across Sixth Avenue to Trinity Presbyterian Church.

Sixth Avenue was the northern border of The Hilltop, one of the roughest neighborhoods of Tacoma. My neighborhood. Shotgun Shack sat right on that border. Then came a triangular block called The Wedge, which, like the name said, was wedged between Sixth Avenue and Division Street. On the northern side of The Wedge, across Division, was The North End, the wealthy part of town where families like the Lears lived.

The Wedge was a transition neighborhood—a zone of truce between rich and poor, black and white. Trinity Church formed the very tip of The Wedge, right between The Hilltop and The North End. The people who attended Trinity either lived in The North End, where houses were overpriced, or lived on the edge of The Hilltop, where beautiful old homes were cheap and dreams of upward mobility survived, despite the empty forty-ouncer bottles strewn along the sidewalks.

Trinity was a small church—the sanctuary could hold about two hundred people, but the few times I'd been there it had no more than one hundred twenty, including children. It was usually a pretty busy place all week long, though, with afterschool programs, Alcoholics Anonymous meetings, a soup kitchen, a clothing bank, and a once-a-week medical clinic where I'd always gotten my shots for measles and mumps.

The sanctuary had seen better days. It looked at least a century old, with stained-glass windows, ornate masonry work, and a ceiling that must have been thirty feet high. But the masonry was crumbling, the ceiling leaked, and the stained glass had holes from the BB guns of the neighborhood.

The sanctuary was dark now. I tried the door handle, but it was locked. A keyhole looked at me from below the handle. That's when I realized I had Mom's key ring. As a cleaning woman, she had keys to all of the businesses she worked for.

That meant that I could open any of those locks, whenever I wanted.

Instead of using one of Mom's keys, I walked to the church office, which sat in a little house next door. I could see a woman inside, so I knocked and went in. The woman sat at a desk behind a nameplate that read Diane Niebauer. Diane was pretty and plump, her straight blond hair cut short and neat. I guessed that she was forty years old. She wore a too-tight tan business suit. I bet Diane had bought the suit on sale, with plans of losing weight, then just said *screw it*.

"Can I help you?" asked Diane as she smiled.

"I was hoping to talk to Pastor Vandegrift."

"Oh, honey, he's not here. He's visiting Mrs. Prentice in the hospital. But I could take a message for him."

"Umm. Okay. Could you tell him that Seth Anomundy came by?"

Diane's smile fell away. "Oh, my dear, you must be Eve's son. Oh, my dear." She stepped up from her chair and came around the front of her desk and pulled me into a squishy hug. "Oh, honey." She stepped back. Her eyes were brimming with tears, but she dabbed them away with a Kleenex before they ran down her perfect makeup. "I'm so sorry. I'll be sure to tell Pastor V you stopped by. He'll want to talk to you."

"That would be great, because I'm investigating who might have murdered my mom."

Diane suddenly looked like she'd drunk bad communion wine. "You want to talk to the pastor about murder?"

"Yes. My mom's."

She walked back behind her desk and sat down in her chair. "I don't know what you might hope to learn from our pastor. He's a good man."

"I'm sure he is. I just want to talk to him."

"Why don't you just talk to me and leave him out of it?"

I stood there silently and smiled as politely as I could stand to.

"You're upset," Diane said. "I suppose I can pass your number on to him." I told her the number to my cell phone. She wrote it down slowly on a sticky note. "Anything else?"

I was pretty sure I wouldn't see any more smiles from Diane, so I said no. Diane's response didn't bug me. She loved her boss and was looking out for him. And for all I knew, he probably *was* a good man. Diane was protecting her own. I wished I had someone like her in my life, looking out for me.

I started to leave when Diane stopped me. "Oh, Seth, I actually have a question for you. Would you be interested in cleaning the church like your mom did? We're a bit desperate. And we'd pay you the same as we paid your mom."

I thought about it for a few seconds. Should I feel complimented because she trusted me enough to work alone in the sanctuary, after I'd just asked about a murder? Or should I be pissed off because she thought of my family as nothing more than cleaning people? Either way, I didn't want the job. I said no thanks. There had to be a better way to make a living than cleaning up after church kids.

Ten

While I was walking back to the Jeep, my phone rang. It was
Ms. Edelson, my high school counselor. She apologized for
taking so long to get in touch with me, but she'd thought I
might need a few days to sort stuff out. "You and I need to
talk, Seth. We need to come up with a plan."

"I'd like to have a plan," I said. I agreed to come and see
her the next day, Friday, at two o'clock.

I'd had enough investigating for a while, so I left the church
and went to another spiritual place—King's Books, a sprawling used bookstore on St. Helens Avenue—to hang out with
Sweet Pea, the red-haired man who seemed to work at the
store twelve hours a day, seven days a week. Sweet Pea had
taken the store over from its original owners and turned it
into a dog-eared Mecca for booklovers.

King's was a maze of pinewood bookshelves with handwrit-
ten section labels—history, mystery, literature, self-help. Miko,
the bookstore cat, was a twenty-pound gray tabby who could
rub hard enough against a pant leg to remove the cords from
corduroy. Other than the shelves, the store was furnished with
mismatched antique tables and slightly uncomfortable chairs.

"You don't want them too comfortable," Sweet Pea had told me once, "or some customers might never leave."

Sweet Pea was a tall, skinny, Irish-American with a tendency to wear his tomato-soup-red hair in pigtails and to dress in vintage rodeo shirts. He balanced his outrageous style with a black belt in Kung Fu, an astonishing knowledge of literature, and a hand-picked selection of graphic novels—my personal favorite section of the store. When I went in this time, Sweet Pea's shirt looked like a bright-red version of a Civil War uniform. He had a short line of buyers at his counter.

"Mr. Pea," I said in greeting.

"Mr. Anomundy."

"Got any graphic novels I should shamelessly read without buying?"

"Maybe. Did you like that Jacques Tardi I showed you last time you were in here? We just got another one in. It's on the *featured* table. I'll be over there in a minute."

Tardi is a French guy who made most of his graphic novels in the 1970s. I read one by him called *West Coast Blues* about this average family man who is sucked into a circle of war criminals and assassins. Tardi's drawings look like black-and-white versions of TinTin comics, but in Tardi's books, people get shot, bleed, and die.

The one I saw now was called *It Was the War of the Trenches*. It looked like something about World War Two or some other ancient conflict. I thumbed through its pages of hand-drawn violence until Sweet Pea ambled over.

"Tardi is a master, isn't he?"

"I liked that last one you sold me," I said, "but this one looks a bit too much like a history lesson."

"World War One. The bloodiest of them all. You need to

learn to embrace a little history, Anomundy. The goriest gore happens in real life."

"Never really took you for a history buff, Mr. Pea."

"Oh, hell yeah. You think all I read is the made-up stuff? Not that half of history isn't made up, too, but like they say at the beginning of movies, it's based on a true story."

I bought the Tardi and took it home. I lay on Mom's daybed until dinnertime, reading the book all the way through and then halfway through again, interrupted only by the school computer, calling to tell me I missed school again.

A couple of hundred people died on those pages. I was strangely comforted by the thought of other people dying. Death wasn't just something that happened to my family. Death transformed normal kids like me into orphans all over the world.

It reminded me of a song by the Flaming Lips. I found it and played it on my crappy old iPod. The Lips sang soft, sad, and slow and I played the song over and over.

Do you realize
that you have the most beautiful face?
Do you realize
we're floating in space?
Do you realize
that happiness makes you cry?
Do you realize
that everyone you know someday will die?

At six o'clock, I headed back to Shotgun Shack. I stared through the restaurant windows for a glimpse of Miss Eye. She wasn't there. King George's black BMX bike was propped against the wall.

I walked inside. Stanley Chang was missing again. In the corner, King George leaned over his table, sawing through a big rib-eye steak with a butter knife. Facing him, with his back to me, was a small man I didn't recognize at first. Then the man tilted his head in a familiar way. It was Nadel. I'd never seen him in Shotgun Shack before. Why would he come here? Nadel was as meticulous about his food as he was about everything else. He was a health nut. He ate vegetarian, and Shotgun Shack was all about pig fat and catfish.

The old man and the young man were deep in conversation, so I studied them without their noticing. Even from the back, Nadel was precise. He had only coffee and toast before him, but I could see him dissect his toast carefully with the side of his fork. He was a small, old man in every way—thin wrists, thin neck, and narrow head covered in thinning hair.

Facing him, King George was his opposite. His teenaged muscles bulged, his voice was loud, and either of his hands looked like they could crush Nadel with a twitch of thick fingers.

There were no vacant tables, so I went back into the kitchen, where Checker was cooking and cursing. He asked if I wanted to grab an order pad and start waiting on customers. I said no, but I'd cook. Checker nodded, gave me his apron, and went out into the dining room to calm down the impatient diners.

The stack of orders was high. I grabbed the first one, which called for a chicken-fried steak and a side of corncakes. That sounded good to me, so I made two of the steaks and two orders of cakes. I set one steak and cakes up on the order window and ate the other. Then I began filling orders as fast as I could. I grew faster as the night wore on, noticing that some of my movements—the way I breaded the catfish in cornmeal and the way I pulled biscuits from the oven—were the same movements I'd seen Miss Irene do over the years. I still wasn't near as fast as she was, but I was improving. The trick, I realized, was to channel Miss Irene.

Three hours and dozens of orders later, Checker Cab locked the door behind the last customer, flipped the closed sign, and dimmed the lights. Instead of thanking me, he said, "Now what? I got all this mess and your mom's not here to clean it up. What am I s'pposed to *do*?"

I told him to go home and go to bed. He gave me five twenty-dollar bills and left while I stayed behind and cleaned. It took me three hours—at least two hours longer than I thought it would. I wiped, swept, mopped, scraped, soaked, washed, and rinsed. It was near midnight when I locked up and left.

I was tired of cleaning and tired of thinking about Mom while I cleaned. I knew she was better at this kind of work than me. She would have laughed at the way I'd swept the floor before wiping off the tables, which meant I had to sweep twice. My one night of cleaning the restaurant taught me how hard she'd worked every night for all my life.

Even though I was beat, I didn't feel like going home. I drove to Azura's house, got out of Mom's Jeep, and leaned against it. Maybe Azura wanted me, but the rest of the house wished I'd go away. As if in answer to my thoughts, the porch light clicked on and the front door opened. Azura's father stepped into the open doorway, staring my direction. He didn't walk toward me. He didn't even step out onto the porch.

I was tense, standing by Mom's old Jeep, staring at that fancy house. But as he stood on in the doorway of his million-dollar house and stared at my two thousand-dollar car, that rich man seemed at least as edgy. I slowly realized that Azura's dad was afraid of me. I smiled. I was an unknown quantity to him. He came from a world of neckties until five o'clock and polo shirts until ten, while I walked around in sagged jeans and wifebeaters. His world was all conversations and cocktails.

Mine was fistfights and forty-ouncers. Maybe that's why Mr. Lear hadn't come and talked to me himself. He'd sent four big guys on his behalf. Now he wouldn't even step toward me. I wanted to lunge at this millionaire just to see if he'd flinch.

A part of me wanted to reason with Mr. Lear—to reassure him that I wasn't going to steal his daughter from him. But what could I say that this man would care about? Should I tell him my mom died? That I was turning to Azura for a little comfort? That she might be turning to me for the same thing? He'd have no sympathy for me and just slightly more for his own daughter. The only thing that might appease Mr. Lear would be for him and me to acknowledge what we both knew—that it wouldn't last. That it didn't matter how much Azura and I connected. That the addresses of our neighborhoods were just too far apart. I wished it wasn't true, then climbed into the Jeep and drove south.

A few blocks later my phone buzzed. I parked, pulled out the phone, and read a text from Azura.

Thanks for coming by.

Almost made it to the front door, I texted back.

Daddy doesn't love you.

I got that sense.

Anyone beat you up because of me today?

Not today, I replied.

I must be losing my touch.

I wouldn't worry about that.

Anything new about your mom?

I texted her about my conversation with Carlyle from the day before, about how Mom was almost certainly murdered—poisoned with cyanide. I told her about Carlyle's certainty of Miss Irene as the prime suspect.

What do you think? Azura asked.

I can't believe Miss Irene would have done it.

Why do the cops suspect her?

Because Miss Eye and Mom were fighting. And because Miss Eye has run away.

Why'd she run?

No idea.

Are you just wishing that she is innocent?

Maybe, I replied. Miss Irene was like a second mother to me. I wanted her back in my life. If there was one woman I'd like to talk to about Mom and about what I should do, it was Miss Eye. I wanted to think she was hurting as much as I was—and missing Mom as much. I needed Miss Irene to be innocent and available.

At ten o'clock the next morning, my phone rang. It was a man named Wayne Carter calling from Allied Allstar Drivers' Academy, one of the businesses Mom used to clean. He said he got my number from my mom's original job application, which listed me as an emergency contact.

"And you have an emergency?" I asked.

"Not in the usual sense," said Wayne, "but my office is a mess and I need someone to clean it. Any chance you'd know someone?"

I lied and said that I might be interested, then lied some more and told him how much experience I had cleaning with my mom. He asked if I could come over and talk to him.

An hour later, I parked in front of the Allied Allstar Drivers' Academy. It was on the north side of Sixth Avenue, about a half mile west of Shotgun Shack, in my favorite part of Tacoma, where restaurants, barbers, coffee shops, and small businesses filled every storefront on both sides of the street for blocks. Allied Allstar was another typical storefront, stuck between a clean tattoo parlor called House of Tattoo and an upscale tavern called Crown Bar. The driving school consisted of a couple of classrooms, a waiting area where some of the furniture actually matched, and a small office behind the reception desk. The door beeped when I stepped inside and a man's voice from the office told me that someone would be with me in just a minute.

While I waited, I looked at a large corkboard hung on the waiting-area wall. The board was covered in photographs and pushpins. Each photo was a picture of a driver standing next to a car and holding a certificate. Most of the drivers were teenagers, looking young, well-groomed, and happy. I'm pretty sure I never looked as young as the kids in those photos.

I searched the photos on the slim chance that I might find a picture of Azura. I found one. I recognized the car first—her shiny Lexus coupe. The photo couldn't be more than a few months old, but the girl looked different than the one I knew—smiling so wildly that I knew she'd been caught in a laugh.

Near the back of the car stood a person that had been cropped mostly out of the photo. It was a woman, but the edge of the photo stopped where her face would have begun. The half-woman was wearing a work uniform, as if she'd just stepped out of her job at a discount department store. Did Azura actually have a friend who held down a retail job? I pulled the photo from the board and slipped it into my pocket.

A few seconds later, Wayne Carter came out from the office with a stack of forms in his hands and a frazzled look on this face. "You can probably see why I called," Wayne said. He motioned around the waiting room, where a trash container was overflowing with candy bar wrappers and crumpled Coke cans. The carpets needed vacuuming. "My customers are mostly high school kids who expect the world to pick up after them. Little slobs."

"My mom cleaned for you every night?"

"Sunday through Thursday," Wayne said. He was a thin man with sharp cheekbones, a messy rim of hair around a mostly bald head and a severe five o'clock shadow. He wore fingerless gloves on his hands and reminded me of Bob Cratchit from *A Christmas Carol*. Wayne held his stack of forms up to his chin for a few seconds. "Listen, kid. I'm really sorry about your mom. If this is too much for you to take on in your what-do-you-call-it—your moment of grief—I totally understand. It's just that I'm a bit desperate."

"Were you here on that last night—the last night my mom cleaned for you?"

"I saw her come in on my way out. We passed each other in the parking lot. Eve was a super nice person, you know? She may have just been the cleaning lady—you understand what I mean when I say that, right?—but she always had a smile on her face. And she always did a little bit extra. Sometimes she'd put fresh flowers on the desk there. And I mean fresh like she picked them from someone's yard that same day, with a few weeds and a few bugs included. Sometimes it was just a little note to me. She ever write you notes? Last week she left me one that said, 'Drive safe. Be sure to check your rearview mirror.' Kinda cute. Maybe a little bit silly. But, you know, every morning, I always looked around the office for one of those notes."

"Did anything seem weird that last night?"

"Hmm. Not sure. Like I said, I just passed her in the parking lot. She still smiled and said hello, but maybe she was a bit off. Like she was tired or something. Was she sick?"

"Not that I know of."

He scrunched up his nose, as if he just smelled sour milk. "Do you, uhh, know what she died of?"

"She was poisoned."

"As in?"

"As in cyanide. As in murdered."

"Jee-zuz. Who would murder a nice lady like that?"

"That's the question. Did you let her into the building?"

"No, she had her own key. I probably need to get that back. You wouldn't know what happened to that key, would you?"

I shook my head no, but could feel the weight of Mom's keychain in my pocket. "Listen," I said, "I don't think I can clean your office for you—"

Wayne frowned. "Oh, no. You sure?"

"—but I might be interested in taking driving classes. How much do they cost?"

The frown crept up toward smile territory. "We're running a special right now for three hundred and forty-five dollars."

"That much, huh?"

"I'll make you a deal if you do some cleaning for me. We could barter. I'm desperate."

"I—I just don't think I'm emotionally ready to take it on. During my moment of grief." I left, got in Mom's Jeep, and drove away. One of these days, I probably needed to get a license.

Eleven

Thirty minutes later, Detective Carlyle called, asking if he could buy me lunch. At my suggestion, we met at Pho Bac for more noodle soup. Carlyle and I arrived at the same time. We took a table against the wall, below a brown-toned oil painting that I always assumed was a herd of stampeding horses. It was hard to be sure. The painting looked like it was accidentally abstract.

Mae, one of the tiny women who ran Pho Bac, brought two small porcelain cups and a stainless steel pot of tea to our table. "Hi Seth. How are you today?"

"I'm okay, Mae, considering. How are you?"

Mae smiled and nodded without answering. She said, "What your friend want?" I shrugged. Carlyle asked what was good and muttered along for a few seconds until I ordered for him. "Give him a small rare and a Vietnamese coffee." Mae nodded and walked away.

"Aren't you eating?" asked Carlyle.

"Mae knows my order."

Carlyle studied the horse painting, then said, "When I was your age, I always thought it would be cool to become a regular at a restaurant. So that when I walked in, the waiter would say, 'Hey, Carlyle, you want your same-old today?' I'd nod and the waiter would bring me my food—maybe even sit down and join me for a meal every now and then. I've gone to the same diners and the same bars ever since, ordering the same crappy food every time I go in. I've been going to the Breakneck Bar and Grill on South Twelfth for at least ten years. Every time I go in, I get a mushroom burger with no mayo and a side salad with blue cheese dressing. That's it. I've ordered that same mushroom burger and side salad at least a hundred times. But each time I walk in, it's like I've never been there before. They still screw up the mayo at least half the time. And I don't want ranch dressing. I want blue cheese. Now here you are—how old are you? Sixteen? And you're already such a regular here that they don't even ask what you want. They just bring it." He looked at the painting again. "Not that this is much of a restaurant."

I shrugged. "Wait until you taste the soup."

"Okay. Okay. Fair enough." Carlyle slowly poured out two cups of tea. "Seth, I'm getting the feeling you're not taking my advice."

I sipped my tea.

Carlyle continued: "I asked you not to get involved with your mom's investigation. Against my better judgment, I even did what you requested—I went around personally to all the other businesses your mom worked at that last night, to see if there was any chance another suspect might show up—one that might somehow—in some miraculous way—look like a better suspect than Irene Dunlop. Guess what I found out?"

I took another sip of tea, because I didn't know what else to do.

"I found out that I wasn't the only one asking around,"

Carlyle said. "Turns out another detective is on the case. One that would be better off if he went back to school."

Between sips, I said, "You must mean either Dix or Chambers. Both of those guys could benefit from a little continuing education."

"No argument. But Seth, you need to stay out of this thing. This is serious business. Your mom was murdered. Whoever did that has already proved they're capable of taking a life. They're going to be desperate. And they're going to be dangerous."

"I can take care of myself."

"No doubt you think you can. But this isn't some dust-up on the playground. This is homicide."

"I get it. So what'd you find?"

Carlyle frowned. "I found that your mom cleaned the church as scheduled, then went to the driving school, then Shotgun Shack, then on to Nadel's clock shop, all as scheduled. Then she was seen leaving Nadel's clock shop, as witnessed by the bartender at the tavern across the street. I found that she was seen earlier in the evening having a heated argument with Irene Dunlop at Shotgun Shack. I found that she'd had numerous arguments with Irene Dunlop over recent months, some of them described as, and this is a quote, 'vicious as two alley cats.' I found that Irene Dunlop has still not been seen since the day following the murder—that she insomuch as abandoned the restaurant she worked at nearly every day without fail for more than a dozen years."

My cell phone rang. I ignored it. "She'll show up."

"I hope you're right. Because when she does, we'll arrest her. We've issued an APB for her arrest. She's our suspect, Seth. All signs point to her. Sorry if that's hard for you to hear, but that's simply the way this one is going. I've been a cop for almost twenty years and this is as clear-cut a case as I've seen. Irene Dunlop killed your mom."

"No, she didn't."

"You are a young man of great faith. I can appreciate that. But I've got a nose for this kind of thing and my nose is certain about this one."

Mae came over to the table with two steaming bowls of soup, but I'd suddenly lost my appetite.

"So that's that," said Carlyle. "And it also means you get possession of your mother's remains."

I left the restaurant, wondering whether or not Miss Irene was guilty and wondering what the hell I was supposed to do with the remains of my mother—the hundred-or-so pounds of flesh and bones—all that was left behind of her complicated life.

Twelve

In Mom's Jeep, I checked the message on my cell phone. It was from Pastor Vandegrift, saying he was available to talk. I drove to the church. Diane Niebauer was wearing a black turtleneck sweater that made her look like a cross between a chubby soccer mom and a commando. "Seth, right?" I nodded. "How are you doing, honey? Stupid question, huh? Pastor V said you might be coming by. Hold on a sec." She spoke briefly into the phone, then smiled toward the pastor's office door.

Pastor Vandegrift stood up from behind an old metal desk when I entered. He was a few inches taller than me and fifty pounds heavier. His hair was black on top and gray on the sides, as if he'd run out of hair dye halfway through the job. His face was red and fleshy. He smiled when I came in. His smile calmed my nerves so much I think I might have sighed out loud.

We exchanged greetings. I told him that I was investigating my mom's death.

"Seems like a good idea." He sat down in his chair and laid both hands flat on his desk, as if he were preparing for me to inspect his fingernails.

"What seems good about it?" I said.

"You're looking for answers. I'm a big fan of looking for answers. That's what I do for a living."

"You found any?"

"I have. Yes. But only a few. Because there are only a few. Everything else is just more speculation and more questions. So you'll have a hard job—this trying to find answers. Needles. Haystacks. All that. But it's still a worthwhile endeavor. And, hey, Seth, even if you don't find anything, I think it will help you come to terms."

"That's not why I'm doing it."

"You may not think so, but it's part of it. Your mom died. She left you alone. You're trying to make sense of the whole thing. Some people go to the family cabin to think about the good old days, some visit monasteries to contemplate God and the universe, some thumb through old photo albums. You investigate your mother's murder. It's really not all that different."

I wanted to shift the conversation. "Did you see her? On her last night?"

"I did, actually. We had an elders' meeting here that evening. It ran late. I was just leaving when I heard Eve's keys in the lock. I opened the door and made her jump. I didn't mean to. Then she came in and I left."

"She say anything to you?"

"Nothing that stands out in my memory. Not that night, at least. On other nights we'd sometimes talk for twenty minutes or more. She was a thoughtful person. Had a point of view on life. And on death, I suppose. We didn't always agree, but I appreciate it when a person at least has a point of view."

"What was hers?"

"Oh, you probably know better than me."

"You might be surprised."

Pastor Vandegrift turned his right hand over and inspected his fingernails on his own. "She said she always tried to live in the here and now."

"In the moment. Yeah, I heard plenty about that."

"It's not far off from what the Bible says, at least in part. *Don't worry about tomorrow, for tomorrow will worry about itself. Each day has enough trouble of its own.*"

"Damn straight."

Pastor V didn't even flinch at my cussword. "I wish I had more to tell you about your mom's death. I'm afraid that's all I know. The church was clean the next morning, so I assume she did her job."

"She always did her job."

"What about you? Who's taking care of Seth?"

"Seth is."

"You're living on your own?"

"I am. I'm old enough that they can't make me live with anyone if I don't want to."

"And you don't want to? Where are you living? Same place?"

"At least for now."

"And what about school?"

"I'm kind of taking a break from school." This got a nervous look from Pastor V. "I might go back, but I need to think about it."

"Think about it. Don't do anything that is going to permanently mess up your future."

"I thought you just told me not to worry about tomorrow."

"Worry about it a little bit."

I smiled. We shook hands and parted. He seemed like a good guy. Maybe he was someone staying clean in a dirty world. I could see why Diane worked to protect him.

I climbed in Mom's Jeep and drove north toward the high school, listening to "Puppets" by Atmosphere on the way.

A lot of pressure in the middle of those shoulders
And we ain't getting nothing but older
Ain't nothing changed but the day we run from
But nobody knows that better than you, huh

I had fifteen minutes before my appointment with Ms. Edelson, the school counselor. I parked outside the southwest entrance of Heath High School. Even though there was still half an hour before the school day ended, a few other cars were already in line—moms and dads talking on cell phones while they waited for their children to come outside. I used to make fun of the kids whose parents picked them up. Spoiled babies. Afraid to walk or ride the bus. Now, I wasn't sure how I felt about them. Jealous, I suppose.

I walked up the stairs to the school's main entrance. I'd been here just a few days ago, but I felt like I was visiting something from my distant past.

It was two o'clock, which meant I was in the middle of the last period. I'd be in Algebra 2 right now, on a normal day, trying to stay focused on quadratic equations. The halls were mostly empty, except for a bored security guard and a few stray students walking around with hall passes. None of them gave me much attention until Patrick Naismith strolled sleepily around a corner with earbuds in his ears. When he saw me, he pulled out a single earbud, but kept nodding loosely to the music playing in his other ear.

"Hey, Seth."

"Hey, Patrick. What're you listening to?" Patrick and I had gone to school together for years. Even in middle school, he'd always hung out with girls more than with boys. He shopped with them, but never dated any of them. The two of us only became friends because of our shared, snobby views about music.

"Radio Moscow. You heard them?"

"No. They any good?"

"Good jams. Not much depth to their lyrics. But if you're in the right mood, you know? They can definitely play. Hey, is it true what I heard?"

"About my mom?"

"No. About you and Azura Lear."

"It might be. What did you hear?"

"That you two were an item. Is it true?"

"I'm not sure. Who'd you hear it from?"

"Janine Turner."

I pulled out the picture of Azura I'd taken from the driving school. "Check this out."

"You carry her picture in your pocket. She's hot, if you're into that. What about it?"

"Any idea who that other person is in the picture?"

"Looks like Azura's mom."

"How can you tell?"

"Azura and I grew up in the same tennis club. Why do you care?"

"Just wondering."

"Speaking of moms, what were you saying about your mom?"

"You didn't hear? My mom died."

Patrick pulled out his other earbud. He said, "Dude." That was the right thing to say.

"It's okay."

"No, it's not."

"Yeah. Anyway, I'm here to talk to a counselor. Trying to figure out what to do about school."

"I bet. Damn. Hey, you want me to burn you a copy of this?"

I said yes, Patrick almost gave me a hug, then didn't. I went on my way.

An office secretary sat me down outside Ms. Edelson's office. I waited ten minutes until some pimply-faced girl exited, avoiding eye contact with me. Ms. Edelson poked her head out. "Seth? Come on in."

Ms. Edelson didn't suck at her job. I'd met with her half a dozen times since my freshman year. She was a straight talker. She knew what was crap and what was actually helpful. And she was honest about the little she could do.

I told her I wasn't ready to come back. She asked how much time I needed. I said I wasn't sure.

She neither smiled nor frowned. "You'll have to talk to each of your teachers. Some are more willing than others to be flexible." She must have seen the desperate look on my face, because she said, "I'll talk to them. Give me your number." She wrote my cell number down on the page of her desk calendar followed by my name and the words, *mother is dead*. On another day she might have written *late for school* or *had his tonsils out*.

She said, "If you miss more than two weeks, we're going to have to look at other options."

"Like what?"

"Hold on. That means, to avoid those other options, you'll need to be back at school Monday after next, at the latest? Think you could manage that?"

"I don't know. What are the other options?"

"First would be summer school. Probably something you don't want to hear. The other would be to transfer to Callison—the alternative high school."

I knew that place. Not that I'd ever been there. But I knew some of the kids who had. King George types, but not so big or mean. Pregnant girls. Kids who'd been to juvie. Most of them seemed to go for a semester or two before they dropped out altogether.

She continued. "It's not as bad as you've heard. But it's not good, either. I think you're better than that, Seth. You've got solid grades for a kid in your situation."

"In my situation?"

"Yes. Don't pretend you're in a good spot. You got a rough deal to begin with and now it's a lot rougher. But don't make it worse by dropping out."

"I get that." I did. Neither one of us spoke for a while. I looked around her office. There were a couple of decent posters on the walls, meaning they weren't pictures of cats and they didn't have motivational slogans on them. Her desk was devoid of any family photos. "Here's the one thing I can't figure out," I said. "If I go to school and do my homework, how do I pay the bills? When do I have time to work? Where do I get the money I need for food or rent?"

She only had a few more ideas than I did. I didn't like any of them. I left, promising I'd at least answer the phone when she called.

Monday after next. Not much time to get life figured out.

I'd promised Azura I'd pick her up after school, so I went outside and leaned against the Jeep. A few minutes later, the last bell rang and students started piling out of doorways. Soon the courtyard was crowded with kids I knew and didn't know. I was scanning the faces of my schoolmates for someone I could legitimately call a friend. Instead, I saw Big Red, Zach, and Cody break through a crowd of kids and swagger over to me. "Why are you here, jackass?" asked Big Red.

I ignored him.

"Thought you would have dropped out by now. Isn't that what kids like you do?"

"Yeah, shouldn't you be gone?" said either Zach or Cody. I couldn't tell which one was which.

"Actually, I'm here to pick up Azura."

"You're what?" said Big Red. "Didn't you get the message the other day?"

"I've always been a little hard of hearing," I said, scanning the crowd for Azura. Maybe this conversation was just banter right now, but it was one word away from a full-on fight.

"Well, even a jackass like you should understand this," said Big Red. Then he pushed me back hard enough to bounce me off the Jeep. Within three seconds, it seemed like every kid in the courtyard started shouting and crowding around us like a feeding frenzy of piranha. Big Red had his hands up and Zach and Cody were leaning and straining toward me, like pit bulls at the ends of their leashes. The rest of the crowd was made up of the loud, leering faces of kids looking excited and hungry, nervous and expectant. I heard Red's name cheered by dozens of them. None of them were saying my name.

A voice shouted above the crowd and Mr. Stevanovich, a weathered teacher and coach, bulled his way through, repeating the words, *break it up, break it up,* over and over again like some sort of incantation. He grabbed Big Red by the collar and told him to clear out or get kicked out. Red glared at me as he turned away and was swallowed by the mob. Then Stevanovich marched right up to my face and hissed, "Your name's Seth, right?"

I nodded.

"You want to keep going to school here?"

I didn't answer.

"School's over. You will either leave now or I will expel you. You have five seconds to make-up your mind. Five, four, three…"

He said the last two numbers to my back. I climbed in the Jeep and drove just off school grounds, parking across the street by the Heath Mart, where underage kids tried to buy beer and cigarettes. I looked in my rearview mirror, wondering if Azura had been part of that swarm of students in the courtyard. Had she stood there, surrounded by all her school friends who were hoping to see me get my butt kicked?

I climbed out of the car to wait for Azura. Thirty seconds later, the twins, Zach and Cody, were on both sides of me. I had no idea where they came from. Erik Jorgensen stepped into view.

"You're persistent, aren't you?"

"I just can't stay away from you, Erik. You're irresistible."

"You should try a little harder. Why are you here?"

"I already told your friends. I'm here to pick up Azura."

"Look, man," said Erik, "I didn't know your mom just died when we came to see you the other day. If I had, I wouldn't have done it. Least not then. But I'm still not gonna sit by and watch you stalk Azura."

Over Red's shoulder, I saw a figure approaching. "You think I'm stalking her?" The figure came closer until I could tell who it was, Azura's dark brown hair in high contrast against her yellow raincoat. "Hi, honey," I said to her. "I wish you'd call when you know you'll be late."

"Sorry, dear. You been waiting long?"

"Long enough to get tossed off the campus. Luckily, these nice young men have been keeping me company."

"And what have the four of you been talking about?"

"Azura," said Erik. "You shouldn't be hanging around this loser."

"Really? Which loser should I be hanging around?"

Erik's face kind of caved in. "Are you serious? I'm trying to look out for you."

"Don't. Just don't." She climbed in the Jeep like she owned it. I bowed politely to each of the twins—I didn't have the heart to do it to Erik—and climbed in after her.

"You practically killed him right there," I said as I turned the key.

She shook her head, but I don't think she was disagreeing with me. Her bangs fell into her eyes and she brushed them away with a manicured hand. "I can't leave you alone for a minute."

"Other than you, trouble is my best friend."

"That was almost sweet."

I told her about my lunch with Carlyle and about the APB on Miss Irene.

"You still think she's innocent?"

"You never met her. She's like a mom to me."

"And you already lost one mom," said Azura.

I told her that Carlyle said I could now pick up my mother's body. "I have no idea what to do about that. How am I supposed to plan a funeral? How am I supposed to pay for it?"

"You're not supposed to," she said. "You've got enough going on. Somebody should handle this for you. Don't you have any family around?"

"No. Mom had some family in Spokane, I guess, but I've never met any of them. I don't even know them."

"What about ChooChoo?"

"What about him? Does he seem like the kind of guy who is good at planning funerals?"

"Who else?"

"No one. You know who I'd call if I could? Miss Eye. She would have taken care of the whole thing—church, food, flowers, and every other detail. She would have demanded that she be the one to do it, because that's how she is. And that's why I don't think she killed Mom. But Miss Eye isn't here, so I'm stuck."

"No, you're not. There's someone else."

"Who?"

"Me. I'll take care of it. Just tell me where you want to have the funeral and I'll figure out the rest. And don't worry about the money." She pulled out a credit card. "This one's on Daddy."

It was the nicest thing anyone had done for me in a long time. I told her so. She kissed me, then kissed me again. That was pretty nice, too.

Thirteen

I asked Azura where she wanted to eat. She said MSM Deli and I almost fell in love. MSM is a sandwich restaurant stuck in the middle of a Sixth Avenue convenience store, but the sandwiches are big, sloppy, and magical. They're served with a quartered dill pickle and wrapped up neat in white butcher paper. Unwrapping the white paper around an MSM sandwich is one of the great pleasures of life in Tacoma and it didn't matter which side of Division Street you lived on. If Azura liked MSM, maybe there was a chance we could last after all.

I picked two orange cream sodas from the cold case and ordered a Mike's Deluxe sandwich—roast beef, cheddar cheese, Swiss cheese, sprouts, lettuce, and onions all falling out from in-between eight-inch slices of fresh French bread. We shared the giant sandwich in the back dining room.

Between bites, she said, "So what about school? When are you coming back?"

"I talked to Ms. Edelson. She said by the latest I have to be back by Monday after next."

"So this coming Monday?"

"No. The next one. So I can take off next week." I picked up some stray lettuce and ate it. "But I'm not sure I want to go back."

A TV up in the corner was playing local news while we were eating. We both watched it for a few seconds without speaking.

"You have to come back, don't you?"

"I don't have to. I could drop out."

"That seems stupid."

"Maybe. Or maybe not. Maybe I'll be self taught. Like Abraham Lincoln."

"Or Richard Branson," said Azura.

"Who?"

"Richard Branson. Virgin Records. Virgin Atlantic Airlines. He was a high school dropout. Now he's a billionaire."

"Not bad. So yeah, maybe I'll be like Richard What's-His-Face."

"Branson."

"Yeah. Him. And once I'm a billionaire, I won't have to remember people's names."

A grainy, unsmiling photo of Miss Irene appeared on the TV behind the blonde newscaster. It was noisy in the deli and hard to hear, but I could make out something about "wanted in connection with" and "Tacoma-woman, Eve Anomundy."

"So that was a picture of Miss Irene?" said Azura. "She doesn't look very nice in it."

"I recognize that photo. It was on the wall behind the counter in Shotgun Shack. In it, Miss Irene is standing next to a famous blues musician named BB King, because he ate in the restaurant whenever his tour came through town. If you could see BB, you'd see a huge smile on his face. Checker Cab used to tease Miss Eye about how grumpy she looked in that photo. She'd say, "That's because while you were trying to figure out how to use the camera, my biscuits were burning."

"I guess it's hard to tell what someone is like from a photograph," said Azura.

I remembered the picture of Azura I stole from the driving school. I pulled it out of my pocket. "Like this photo here," I said. "The girl in this photo looks like she doesn't have a care in the world. But the girl across the table from me seems as weighed down as I am."

Azura grabbed the snapshot. "Where'd you get this?" She smiled as she studied the photo for a moment, then ran her finger along its edge, tempting a paper cut.

I said, "It's a good picture of you, in front of your fine automobile. Who's standing at the back of the car? Your mom?"

She didn't answer. Her smile drifted away, but she kept staring. I repeated the question. "How'd you know?" she said.

"I guessed. She as nice as your dad?"

"They're divorced. She flew up from California to take me for my test. She lives in Sacramento. I don't see her much. But she's nice. I miss her like crazy."

"What's she wearing? In the picture."

Azura ignored my question. "I called her at work that morning. Dad was supposed to take me to my driving test, but like always, he made plans that didn't include me. I was mad. We'd already missed one test and it would take a month to schedule another appointment. So I called Mom, not to ask her to come, but just to talk to someone, you know? She asked what time my appointment was. I told her four o'clock. She shows up at the house at three to pick me up. She left work without changing her clothes, drove straight to the airport, and flew up here, just so I would still make the appointment. I passed the test. We took the photo. Then we went out for dinner on Dad's credit card. It was one of the best nights ever."

"That's pretty nice, all right. Where's she work?"

"Donner's Lumber and Hardware. She's just a regular old store clerk. First real job she's ever had in her life."

"Funny, but you don't strike me as the daughter of a store clerk."

"Dad divorced her. He has better lawyers than she does. She got nothing. Not even visitation rights. So she moved in with her parents—my grandparents—down in Sacramento. She got a job at a local hardware store. She says she loves it—the job, I mean. I believe her."

"But you're up here and she's down there."

"Meaning?"

"I don't know. Doesn't she want to be near you?"

"I think she does. I mean, she does, but she can't afford it. And I think she really wants to be away from my dad."

"So she wants to be away from him more than she wants to be near you?" Azura didn't answer that one. She said: "What time is it?"

"Why?"

"Because it's Friday. And I promised Janine I'd go to her party. Remember—*all the phonies in one room.* I said I'd bring you."

"I'm not going."

"Why not?"

"You go. I'll be okay." I smiled without feeling. "What was the deal?"

"What deal?"

"I mean, why'd they split up? Your parents."

"Depends who you ask. Dad says that Mom's personality wasn't conducive to my self-esteem. Mom says that Dad didn't think she measured up."

"They kind of sound like the same thing."

"Hmm. Maybe they are. Anyway, Dad comes from this snooty East Coast family. He tracks his ancestors back to the revolutionary war and that sort of thing. His great-great-

great-great grandfather or whatever was George Washington's aide. In fact, that's why you came to the house. Some fancy East Coast member of the Lear family died and left Dad that clock you picked up from us. It's a bazillion years old, just like most of the stuff in our house."

"Yeah, Nadel was gushing over how rare it was." An idea struck me. "How much you think that clock is worth?"

"I have no idea. A lot probably. Maybe fifty thousand. Why? You think Nadel would murder your mom to get a clock?"

"Man loves his money, but he's always been like family to us. Anyway, that makes no sense. It's your dad's clock. Your dad knows where it is. There's no reason my mom would even be involved." I tore the dill pickle in two and ate my half. "Your mom into antiques, too?"

"Mom's family is significantly less snooty."

"Then why'd your parents get married in the first place?"

"They met in college. Mom was a scholarship kid at Penn State and Dad went there because all his male ancestors went there, back into the 1800s. Mom says that once upon a time, she and Dad were actually in love. Dad's parents never approved because they'd never heard of her family. So, at the end of Mom's sophomore year in college, Mom and Dad ran out west together. That's how they landed here. But Dad eventually came around to his parents' way of thinking. So now Dad and I live alone in this big fancy house and mom lives alone in Sacramento."

"I thought you said she lived with her parents."

"She does. She lives alone with her parents. Just like I live alone with my dad."

"So why don't you go to California and stay with your mom?"

"Because Dad has custody."

"So what? You're sixteen. In this state, that means you can decide for yourself. That's why I can live alone and not with a foster family. If I were you, I'd just run away and move in with my mom."

"It's easy to say."

"Yeah, especially when it means you'd have to be the daughter of a store clerk."

"You think that's why I'm up here?"

"I think that's part of it. I mean, if I had to choose between a nice house and living with my mom, I wouldn't hesitate."

"You can be a real jerk sometimes."

"That's why you love me."

"It's not funny. You are not funny." She took a bite of her sandwich and glared at me. I took a bite of mine and stared back. I tried to look as serious as possible. She held my stare, then finally broke into a partial smile. "You should be nice to me, you know. I'm planning your mom's funeral."

"You're right. I'm sorry. I've just never been very good at nice. But for you, I think I could learn." I went to the counter for a few extra napkins. When I came back I said, "Question: Who bought your car for you? The one in the picture."

"My dad. Why?"

"Because it's complicated, that's why."

"What is?"

"Parents. Moms. Dads. They are just so damn complicated."

Fourteen

I stared out the window of MSM, but all I could see was my own reflection. There I was, sitting at the table with this beautiful rich girl who I'd deeply known for only a handful of days.

Soon Mom would be buried in the ground somewhere. I'd be alone in our crappy little apartment. I kept expecting Mom to come home. I kept thinking that I'd go back to ChooChoo's gym and she'd be upstairs, waking up from a nap, giving me a present, sharing some advice she'd never figured out how to follow on her own. But she wasn't coming back. I was alone for good.

I looked at Azura. Was there any chance this girl could be a part of my life? It seemed so unlikely. I'd never been good at making friends. I'd never had much of a girlfriend before. Now this one comes into my world right when I need her the most. Would she be gone in a week? Would she last a month? What then?

I drove Azura to her car, which she'd parked near the school. Before she got out of the Jeep, she turned to me. "Come to the party with me."

"Not tonight."

"I don't want you to be alone."

"I don't want to be."

"Then come with me."

"I'll be fine. That's what I'm supposed to say, right?"

"You're supposed to tell the truth."

"Mom always said, if you haven't got something nice to say—"

"It's fine to be sad. It's natural."

"It sucks."

"I've got to go. I promised."

She left to join her friends. I went back home and went to bed, but I couldn't get to sleep. Mom had worked nights for years, so I was used to being home alone, but the apartment felt particularly empty that night.

I wanted to be with Azura, but I knew where she was and I didn't want to go there. Janine Turner's party.

Janine was a Northeast kid. Northeast Tacoma was a sprawling collection of upscale suburbs that had grown on the edge of the city. Even though it was five miles away, it was still within the Tacoma city limits and Heath was the closest high school, so Northeast kids all made the drive to Heath every morning. I didn't know a single one who took the school bus.

It seemed like all Northeast houses were new. At least they looked new to me. Most of the streets were loops or cul-de-sacs. I'd done a couple of pickups and deliveries for Nadel over there and I got lost every time. Those were the only times I'd been there. I'd heard of the parties thrown by the suburban kids. Some were legendary. But I'd never been invited to one.

I didn't know Janine more than to say hi in a school hall-way, but I understood why Azura liked her. Janine was happy. She almost always smiled. Maybe her life was so perfect that happiness was the natural result. Or maybe she was just wired that way. She had hair so blond it was almost white. She was tall—almost as tall as me—and curvy. I thought she wore braces, but I wasn't sure.

It took me fifteen minutes to drive to her neighborhood and another thirty minutes to find her home. The curving streets seemed to be laid out without logic. The houses all looked almost exactly the same, but a practical builder had plastered oversize wooden house numbers on the fronts, probably recognizing that there was no other way to tell the homes apart.

I finally came upon a street jammed with a lot of parked cars and I saw Azura's Lexus coupe in the mix. Then I just followed the music to the loudest door. Sounded like the Black Keys. At least I approved of that.

I knocked. A tall blond girl who was not Janine opened the door with her back to me. "And I suppose you think you do?" she said, to some unseen person behind her. She turned to me and said, "What are *you* doing here?" She gave me a mean stare, then broken into a laugh. "Kidding. C'mon in. I like your shirt. Makes you look all gangster." She walked unsteadily back into her unfinished conversation, leaving me to close the door.

I stepped into the house. Dozens of shoes were piled next to the front door, but I decided to keep mine on. Didn't want anyone stealing my new LeBrons.

Boys and girls stood around in clusters. A few looked in my direction and nodded. I knew a lot of the names, but didn't know any of the people well enough to know which ones could help me find Azura. I walked through an archway into the living room.

A pile of girls and one guy covered a couch, twisted together like the arms of an octopus. "Seth!" the guy shouted, from the middle of the pile. "Twice in one day, brother." It was Patrick. Having him speak my name calmed my nerves.

"Hey, Patrick. This your mix coming through the speakers?"

"How'd you know?"

"Because it doesn't suck."

Patrick laughed, then dug his way out of the female arms and legs. He stood up. "What're you doing here, dude? Didn't think this was your scene."

"Is it yours?"

He laughed again. "You know what? I think it is. These people depend on me. I bring a little light into their darkness."

"Or at least you bring a little B.S."

"That too, dude. What's up with you?"

"I'm looking for Azura. Saw her car out front."

"Serious? So it is true. You two are an item. She doesn't seem like your scene, either."

"Not sure yet. You know where she is?"

"I don't. Maybe in the back. See ya." He dove back into all that flesh on the couch. The girls there giggled.

I walked through the doorway into a large, bright kitchen. On the counter was an arrangement of bottles—wine, beer, vodka, tequila, and a few more caramel-colored liquids I didn't recognize. Four boys were liberally pouring shots for the unsteady blonde who had opened the front door. I walked by and exited onto a back patio.

The backyard lights were off. A few couples were jammed into patio chairs, talking, drinking, and making out. One girl looked up when I walked by, then went back to her business. I saw Azura and another girl that I thought was Janine at the far end of the deck, in what looked like a deep conversation. Azura glanced up when I approached.

"Seth, what are you doing here? What's wrong?"

"Nothing. I came to be with you."

"You did? Really?"

"Really. You think I'd come for another reason?"

She frowned at me. "This is Janine. She looked at her friend. "Janine, this rude boy is Seth Anomundy."

"Hi," said Janine. She smiled. I was right about the braces. Even in the dark, I could see the teeth beneath them were still crooked, but I bet her parents and her orthodontist would pull them into shape. The rest of her was perfect already.

"Hi," I said. I turned to Azura. "You wanna get out of here?"

"Maybe in a while, but not yet. Sit down and talk to us for a few minutes."

I sat down, but nobody talked. Finally, Janine said, "This is fun." She almost sounded like she meant it.

I thought about leaving, with or without Azura.

Patrick came stumbling through the deck door and hustled over to us. "Hey, Seth. Erik Jorgenson just got here."

I jumped to my feet. Azura stood up next to me and put a hand on my shoulder. "Stay. I'll go talk to him. Just wait for me here."

"I'll go with you," said Patrick.

I stood and watched them disappear through the kitchen doorway. I kept standing.

"You can sit down," said Janine. "She can take care of herself."

I sat, but I kept watching the doorway.

"She told me about you, you know," Janine said.

"Meaning what?"

"Meaning she told me she went out with you. Told me you came to her house after your mom—she didn't hide it or anything."

"So she wasn't ashamed of me?"

"Right."

"How brave of her." I worked hard to let my sarcasm show.

We went back to not talking for a while, then Janine said, "It's not that big of a deal."

"What's not?"

"You and her. I mean, she's not my only friend to do this sort of thing."

"What sort of thing is that?"

"I don't know. What would you call it? A bad-boy phase?"

"How long do these phases usually last?"

"The question of the night. For you at least." She stretched out like a cat across her chair, hanging her long legs over the armrest, her arms behind her head. She yawned. "You know, it's like taking your first drink. You're not supposed to do it. Your parents don't want you to do it. You know if they find out they'll be totally pissed off. And it's probably just a bad idea to begin with. But those are all the reasons you do it." She giggled, as if she was remembering something funny.

I looked at her. She looked back and smiled, but kept her lips closed this time. I said, "Here's a question. Would you say you're Azura's best friend?"

Her smiled turned to a frown. "Probably. Why?"

"You'd say she loves you?"

"I guess. Yes."

"Respects you?"

"Respects me?"

"Yes. Do you think she respects you?"

"Respects me? That's a weird thing to ask. Who knows?"

"Not me. I'm gonna go now." I stood up and walked toward the kitchen. I wondered if Prince Erik had his football buddies with him and my fists clenched all on their own. Janine uncurled from her chair and followed me.

Erik and Azura were standing and talking in the middle of the living room. They looked perfect together. Not happy. Just perfect. Fine bloodlines in both families. I tried to guess how the conversation was going, then decided to join it. I walked straight toward them. Erik stopped, turned my direction, and stopped talking in the middle of a sentence. I remembered what a nice swing he had with that baseball bat. My stomach still hurt. He said, "What are you doing here, Seth?"

"Now that is the question of the night." I looked at Azura. "I'm going."

"Just give me a couple of minutes," she said.

"Nah. Take all the time you want, but I'm going now."

"Good idea," said Erik. "Go."

I turned and took a step toward him. I put both my hands on his chest and pushed him, ever so gently. "You bring your bat, Erik? 'Cause I'm happy to stay around and try you without it." He didn't say anything. Patrick and the girls on the couch untwisted themselves to listen. The rest of the room stopped talking, but the music kept pumping. I was half surprised it didn't shut off.

"What do you say, Erik? You want to go outside? Just you and me? Scuffle a little bit?"

He didn't run. But he didn't say a word. I like to believe he looked a little nervous.

So I swung at him, just to make sure. My fist connected with his belly. He wasn't ready for it. He bent over, holding his stomach and moaning. I left. I heard Azura call my name, but I kept walking and she didn't follow.

I drove through those twisting streets for another half an hour, trying to find my way back home.

Fifteen

I stayed in bed until two o'clock the next day. I woke up in a bad mood when ChooChoo knocked on my door and asked me if I was available to spar with his big, dumb prospect, A.J. I said yes and tried to shake the sleepiness out of my head. I was stiff, hungry, and felt like hitting something. Boxing sounded good right then.

I laced up a pair of shoes. ChooChoo helped me into my gloves and headgear. I climbed into the ring with A.J., wondering if ChooChoo had figured out how to break him of his jab-jab-cross habit. I figured there was only one way to find out. We touched gloves and I came right for him. I intentionally gave him an open shot at me, keeping my hands low. He went for it and landed a hook on the side of my head. He had faster hands than I thought. I fell straight down to the mat.

ChooChoo climbed in and checked on me. "Tol' you to spar wit''im, not give 'im target practice. You tryin' t' c'mit suicide?"

I climbed up the ropes to my feet, shook the fuzz out of my brain and faced A.J. This time, I kept my guard up, feeling my way toward him with a few jabs. He jabbed back and I hit him with a jab-cross-hook combination that took him by surprise, landing all three punches but not doing much damage. It made him take me seriously. He came in close and started working on my body—just what he should have done. It hurt. I was still sore from the beating I took from Erik and his friends. I barely made it through the round. When ChooChoo rang the bell, I collapsed in my corner.

ChooChoo was busy giving advice to A.J., so I was on my own. I rinsed out my mouth and toweled the sweat off my face. I tried to get my breath back before my break was over.

When round two started, A.J. went right for my body again. I blocked whatever I could, but enough of his hits still came through that I could barely keep my wind. I was ready to drop.

I'd never even exchanged words with this guy, but A.J. felt like the whole world to me—a world that was bigger, meaner, and stronger than me. I was lined up for another ass-kicking when what I really wanted was to kick ass.

Somewhere down deep, I found a crumb of strength and broke away from A.J. I danced across the ring from him, trying to catch my breath. He must have known that I was just one good punch from going down. He came at me swinging. I countered, somehow, with a couple of decent body blows. That was all it took for A.J. to fall into his old, bad habit. Jab, jab, cross. It was like a tic with this guy. I blocked his first combination without much trouble, except he punched so hard it hurt my arm to take the hits.

The next time he came at me, I ducked under his cross and hit him with a solid uppercut to the chin, then two more quick punches that actually sent him back against the ropes. He shook them off, then came at me again. I did the exact same thing—ducked his punch and threw an uppercut to his chin. With gloves on and with my skinny arms, I wasn't doing a lot of damage, but I could tell I was pissing A.J. off. He came at me again, swinging wildly, and I hit him twice more. He was windmilling like an overgrown sixth-grader and I was ducking under his punches and countering with quickness and precision. A.J. kept getting angrier and I wasn't letting up.

After one of A.J.'s wild swings, I got off a hard three-punch combination that stunned him. We were only sparring, so I should have backed off, but I was raging by now and I just kept hitting until I had him back against the ropes. I hit him until he would have fallen down, but the ropes kept him up and I kept swinging.

I could hear ChooChoo's voice one hundred miles away yelling for someone to stop doing something. I could hear another voice, too, but this one was screaming in animal noises and sobs.

That was me.

ChooChoo pulled me off A.J. and he fell to the mat. ChooChoo held me by my shoulders as I kept swinging at the air, kept growling and sobbing. Finally, he let me fall to the mat, too.

I crawled out of the ring and upstairs to my apartment, where I unlaced my gloves with my teeth and sat in the shower until the water ran cold. I turned the TV on to some droning voices, then buried my head in a couch pillow.

For the next two days, I barely came off that couch. I ate food every now and then, slept off and on and stared right through the TV. I could hear my phone buzzing, letting me know that someone was texting me, but I never checked to see who it was.

Finally, on the morning of the third day, ChooChoo rolled the stone away from my grave and pulled me to my feet. Azura was standing behind him, with a dry-cleaned suit draped over her arm. ChooChoo left.

"It's today," Azura said, handing me the clothes.

I showered and shaved. I put on a clean t-shirt and boxer shorts, then climbed into the black pants and white shirt Azura gave me. I had no idea what to do with the tie, so I came out and told Azura so.

"Come here," she said. She flipped up the collar of my shirt and wrapped the tie around my neck, with the fat end hanging farther down. She wrapped the fat end once around the skinny end and pulled it over the front of the knot, letting it fall to the back. Then she wrapped it around to the back once more, brought it over the top and somehow slipped it through the knot. She buttoned the top button of my shirt, then pulled the tie up tight.

"Put the jacket on," she said. I draped it over my shoulders. She adjusted my shirt cuffs and smoothed down the front of the jacket. "You look better than you have a right to, you jerk. I bet your mom would love to see you dressed up like this."

I tried to say thank you, but words weren't quite yet ready to form in my mouth.

Azura kissed me on the cheek, more like a mother than a girl. "This day is about your mom. Go do this for her."

Sixteen

The funeral was held graveside at a cemetery in Lakewood, one town south of Tacoma. I parked Mom's Jeep on a curving cemetery lane and Azura and I walked through the tombstones marking the burial sites of hundreds of other people's dead parents and children. *Do you realize that everyone you know someday will die?*

There were about forty people gathered at Mom's gravesite, which surprised me. What surprised me even more was that I knew nearly all of them. Most of Mom's customers were there—Pastor Vandegrift and Diana from Trinity Presbyterian Church, Wayne from the driving school, Checker Cab from Shotgun Shack. Stanley Chang—wearing a black suit over a plain, black shirt—and a few other Shotgun Shack regulars stood in a group at the foot end of the casket, comforting each other. I recognized some of Mom's old customers as well, like Mrs. Tavish, who used to hire Mom to clean her house until Mrs. Tavish was laid off from her office job because she was so old and tired she couldn't stay awake at work. Mom kept cleaning it for a while for free, until Mrs. Tavish made her stop. Javier Montero, who ran the muffler shop right next to Shotgun Shack, was another former customer. He was there with his wife, who was swathed in black lace from head to waist and blue jeans and sneakers from the waist down. Javier finally stopped using my mom as a cleaning lady when he realized that his customers didn't care if his shop was clean and he didn't either. ChooChoo was there, with a small crowd of boxing folks. Manny the trainer; A.J., who stayed away from me; and a handful of other fighters and trainers. Sweet Pea and Nikki came together, even though neither one had ever met my mom. Nikki gave me a hug, and almost smiled at Azura. The rest of the crowd were those vaguely familiar people I knew from the neighborhood—the people whose names Mom always reminded me of, but that I couldn't remember that day.

Detective Carlyle was there. At first, his presence made me mad. But he didn't try, even for a second, to conduct any business. He wore a suit, but he was still the worst-dressed man at the place.

Seeing that crowd finally loosened my tongue. "Thank you," I said to Azura, who was holding on to my arm. The crowd loosened my eyes, too. Tears started rolling down my cheeks, one after another. I let them flow.

All the mourners looked like they were genuinely sad that my mom had died. Either that, or they were simply considering their own mortality. Funerals have a way of reminding you that your days are numbered.

The weather held while Pastor Vandegrift gave a short talk. He spoke for a while about there being a time for everything. He reminded everyone that Jesus went to heaven before the rest of us, so he could get the place spiffed up for the arrival of people like my mom. "I go there to prepare a place for you." That's what Jesus said, according to Pastor Vandegrift. He kind of made Jesus sound like a cleaning lady.

The pastor finished strong. At the close of his talk, he said, "Eve and I had one common interest: Poetry. Our tastes were different, perhaps. I was more Carl Sandberg and she was more Khalil Gibran, but still, it seemed appropriate to me that I share a poem today. I'm certain that the one I chose would not have been a favorite of Eve's. It's a war poem. It's about soldiers, not mothers. But I think you'll get the idea. It's by Archibald MacLeish and was written at the very outset of World War Two.

And then he read:

The young dead soldiers do not speak.
Nevertheless, they are heard in the still houses:
who has not heard them?
They have a silence that speaks for them at night and
when the clock counts.
They say: We were young. We have died. Remember us.
They say: We have done what we could but until it is
finished it is not done.
They say: We have given our lives but until it is finished
no one can know what our lives gave.
They say: Our deaths are not ours; they are yours;
they will mean what you make them.
They say: Whether our lives and our deaths were for
peace and a new hope or for nothing we cannot say;
it is you who must say this.
They say: We leave you our deaths. Give them their
meaning.
We were young, they say. We have died. Remember us.

Azura and I left at the first pitch of earth into the grave. I didn't want to stick around and figure out how I was supposed to reply to all the sympathy people were waiting to pour out on me.

It was quiet in the car. I had the radio switched off. Azura's hand was lightly touching my arm. When I realized it, I covered her hand in mine. We sat like that for fifteen minutes. In my rearview mirror I began to see the other mourners getting in their cars and following each other out of the cemetery. Last to go was Stanley Chang, who climbed into an old, mostly yellow pickup truck, but instead of following the other cars, he turned and drove farther into the cemetery. I watched to see where he went.

"What are you looking at?" said Azura.

"Stanley Chang...is going...why is he going in that direction?" I opened the car door and climbed out. "Are you coming?" I said to Azura.

"I'm coming, Mr. Mood Swing."

We began jogging across the cemetery grounds, running from monument to monument, trying to keep out of sight while keeping up with Stanley's yellow pickup. The truck pulled up in front of a large veterans' memorial and stopped. Azura and I stopped, too, and crouched behind a tombstone. A figure stepped out from behind the memorial. It was a woman in a long-sleeved black dress with a hem that fell all the way to the ground. She was wearing a wide-brimmed hat with a facial veil so that it was impossible to see any part of her face, hair or skin. Stanley jumped out of his truck and opened the passenger door. The woman stepped inside. Stanley closed the door, got in on his own side, and drove away.

Azura and I ran back to the Jeep, but by the time we got there, the yellow truck was gone.

"Who was that lady?"

"Who do you think?" I said.

Seventeen

Azura texted me the next afternoon, asking if I wanted to run an errand with her. She drove over and picked me up in her Lexus at three o'clock. Her iPod was plugged into her car stereo, playing Jack Johnson again. I scrolled through her playlist and switched it to Kid Cudi without asking. She frowned at me, so I switched it back. "Where are we going?" I asked.

"Does it matter, as long as you're with me?"

"I guess that depends on where we're going." She frowned again, then explained that her dad had asked her to pick up the antique clock from the repair shop. I frowned back at her. She noticed.

"What's wrong?"

"Nothing. It's just that Nadel usually asks me to do pickups and deliveries for him. Wonder why he didn't call me."

"Maybe he heard how you pick up more than just clocks. You pick up daughters, too."

"I thought *you* picked *me* up."

"That's what you want to think. You picked up precisely what you needed."

"Does your dad know you're with me?"

"No. I lied and said I'd do it by myself."

Azura's answer bugged me. I was the boy she had to lie about.

In a dirty world, what's the point of being clean? What was the point? Everyone was dirty in some way. Miss Irene said she was innocent of Mom's murder, but then she ran from the cops. Checker Cab was still holding down the fort, but he was probably skimming off the till as well. Everybody had an angle. Did Azura have one, too?

"This guy was one of your mom's customers?" asked Azura.

"Nadel? Yeah. One of her oldest. I've been hanging out in his shop for pretty much my whole life. He's a funny old guy, but always been nice to me."

The bell on the door dinged when we entered the shop. "Just a minute," Nadel called from the back.

The shop was full of clocks, all running simultaneously. Big grandfather clocks with lazy pendulums, small dome clocks with spinning weights under glass, shelves of mantle clocks, walls of wall clocks, a case full of antique wrist and pocket watches. All were running.

"I wonder what time it is," I said.

Azura rolled her eyes, then went back to staring around the room. "It's like Gepetto's," said Azura, "in *Pinocchio*. It's only ten minutes until the top of the hour. Will they all start gonging then?"

"Oh, yeah. Nadel always keeps them all running. He says that's the only way to display a clock and the only way to make sure it's still working well. Nadel says that anything mechanical will break down eventually. But that anything broken can be fixed. And believe me, this guy can fix anything."

"I want to stay until they all go off," Azura said.

"Then we'll stay. C'mon," I said. "Let's go into the workshop. It's pretty cool back there, too." I led Azura around the counter and through the workshop door. Nadel was just finishing cleaning the floor—sweeping a neatly mounded pile of dirt into a dustpan. He didn't notice us.

The workshop was as clean as I'd ever seen it, with all the drawers and cupboards closed. The Lear clock was hanging on the wall, just as it had been since the first day it arrived. The only other clock in the workshop was a humble little Hermle regulator which had been bouncing around his store forever. The workbench was bare, except for Nadel's drill press, vice, and other tools. Two books were opened on the workbench as well. Manuals, maybe? I'd never seen books in the shop before, so I had no idea what they might be.

"Hey, Nadel," I said. "Hope it's okay that I let Azura come back here."

Nadel froze in mid-sweep. He dropped the broom and spilled the contents of the dustpan, sending sawdust and metal filings across the floor. He stood up. "Seth? What are you doing here?"

"I'm a friend of Azura's. She asked me to come along. We're here for the old clock. For the Lears."

"You two know each other?"

"Yeah, but not for all that long. We actually met when I picked up the clock for you the first time."

"Ahh," he said. "That's interesting." He was still wiping his hands with the rag, even though they were free of grease. He kept wiping for about ten seconds, then suddenly stopped. He pushed both of us out into the showroom. "Let's talk out here where it isn't so messy." He closed the door behind him. "Your mother. I'm sorry to hear about that."

"Yeah."

"But the clock isn't ready. You'll have to come back later."

"That's weird," said Azura, "because I believe you called our house to say it was done."

"It's not done. Another time. Another time. Good-bye."

He disappeared into the workshop again suddenly.

"What was that about?"

"I don't know. Maybe he's trying to jack up the price of your repair. Nadel likes his money."

"He's definitely a funny old guy. Can we still stay until the clocks go off?"

While we waited for the top of the hour, Azura walked around the showroom, looking at all the old clocks. "That one's a Hayley Perpetual," I said, when she walked up to a six-foot grandfather clock. "It stays wound for eight days and is amazingly accurate, considering it was built more than one hundred and fifty years ago."

"How do you wind it?"

I kind of loved being an expert in her presence. "You pull these chains down, which makes those weights go up. The weights—and gravity—are what power the pendulum. And the pendulum is what powers the gears. Every swing is one click of a gear. And each gear has a different job—transferring power, regulating power, and redistributing power. Some make the hour hand move, some are there for the moon cycle—the part you can see through that little fan-shaped window—and some for the minute hand. They all work together. But when just one tiny part stops working, the whole clock might stop."

We moved silently among the showroom, watching as the minute hands ticked toward twelve. With one minute to go, I heard the workshop phone ring. Nadel's voice said hello, then said, "Why do you keep calling me?" I could only hear his part of the conversation. "He was here... Yes, here in the shop... No, a girl was with him...must be the daughter...yes, what other one would there be? How should I know? I don't think that's necessary. Please stop calling me."

I couldn't hear any more after that, because a small mantel clock near me let loose a soft series of gongs as its hammer clanged against a coil of metal inside. The door of a cuckoo clock next to it opened and the tiny wooden bird poked out and began its mating call. The big Hayley Perpetual took up the low part with its deep, majestic gongs. Three clocks around the shop started playing Westminster chimes, all a half second off from each other, as if they hadn't practiced together before. Before they finished, the whole showroom was gonging, clanging, and chirping. Azura spun around in the middle of it, her arms out, her wide eyes looking from one clock to the next. Then she closed her eyes and listened, her hands turned upward, as if she were standing in the rain trying to catch raindrops. I watched her, thinking how beautiful she was and wondering how Nadel was involved in the death of my mother.

Eighteen

We walked out of Nadel's. Was it possible this old man could be a killer? I didn't think so. I'd always thought of Nadel as a kind of grandfather to me and father to my mom. Now I was wondering if he was a murderer. I was about to get in Azura's car when I noticed the tavern across the street. Breakneck Bar and Grill—the same bar that Carlyle ate in. He'd said the bartender across the street from Nadel had seen my mom leave.

"You thirsty?" I asked Azura. She raised one eyebrow. I'd always wished I could raise just one eyebrow. For me, it was both or nothing.

From the outside, Breakneck Bar and Grill looked like a dump. From the inside, it was one. When Azura and I stepped in, we almost ran into the backs of the three drinkers sitting at the bar, which was less than ten feet from the front door. All three customers turned in unison. They glanced at me for half a second, then slowly ran their gazes up and down Azura. She grabbed my arm as we walked quickly to the end of the bar. I wondered if I made her feel safe.

We sat at two empty stools, next to a dusty jar of pickled eggs and a broken tabletop pull-tab machine. It made me wonder why Carlyle ate here so often, but then in a way it reminded me of him—sleepy, sloppy, and generally unfriendly. The bartender, a short gray-haired man in a dirty yellow t-shirt, slowly worked his way over to us. He smiled. "Gonna have to see your I.D."

"Actually, I just have a quick question for you, assuming you're the bartender that works the late night shift."

"I'm him, but I'm still gonna have to see your I.D. You gotta be twenty-one just to be on the premises."

"We're not twenty-one."

"Then leave." He turned to walk away.

"Just a sec," said Azura. "Could you talk to us outside for three minutes?"

"For twenty bucks, I'll talk to you for two."

I pulled a twenty from my wallet and handed it to the bartender. He turned toward his customers and said, "Jerry, watch the bar for a couple. And keep Albert's greasy lips off the taps." He walked from behind the bar and followed us out. On the sidewalk, he looked at his watch. "The clock is ticking."

"A Detective Carlyle spoke to you recently."

"The cop? About the cleaning lady who was killed? Yeah? So?"

"You told him you saw her leave the clock shop across the street."

"Why are you asking me about this?"

"Because she was my mom."

The bartended raised both eyebrows. Apparently, he couldn't raise only one either. "Your mom? Look—"

"We paid you twenty bucks. You told the cop you saw her leave. Can you tell me what you saw?"

The bartender rubbed the back of his neck. "Look, kid. I, uhh—well, Hell. Okay, I'll tell you the same thing I told that cop. I was cleaning up the place—about three a.m. And

I saw her drive away in her Jeep. I see the same thing at least a couple of nights a week."

"Nothing unusual?"

"Not a thing. Sorry. I wish I could tell you something else."

I thought for a moment. "Did you actually see her walk out of the shop?"

The bartender squinted, then said, "No. I guess not. I only saw her Jeep drive away. But it was definitely her Jeep. I remember because she almost hit a guy on a bike."

"She almost hit a kid?"

"Not a kid. A guy. Big guy on a little bike."

I thought of King George and his huge frame on his BMX bike. "Could you tell if it was her driving?"

"I guess not. It was dark out. I guess I just assumed it was her."

"That's all I need," I said. I thanked him and turned to leave.

"Hey, kid. You should take back your money. I'd feel dirty keeping it." He held the twenty out toward me.

"And I'd feel dirty taking it back from you."

We drove Azura's car toward my apartment. On the way there, my cell phone rang. It was Checker Cab. I let it go to voicemail, because I didn't feel like working the dinner rush that night. When I listened to the message, Checker said he had "some information I might find valuable." We drove over and parked on Sixth.

The restaurant was mostly empty. Two cute teenage black girls I'd never seen before were leaning against the counter, their heads close together in a whisper, as they looked in the direction of King George, who was sitting at his table. Both girls had lots of shiny hair, long, dark eyelashes, and little black aprons over their tight t-shirts and tight jeans. Stanley Chang was in his spot, reading the paper. Azura and I went over to talk to Stanley.

"Hey, Stanley," I said to the old Hawaiian. "Been a while."

"Aloha, cousin," said Stanley. I introduced Azura to him. He asked, "She your *ku`uipo*?" I was pretty sure what that word meant, but I just shrugged.

"Stanley, I'm wondering if you've seen Miss Irene around lately."

Stanley Chang has skin the color of an old wooden floor, but I'm pretty sure he blushed. "Why you asking me?"

I smiled. "Because everyone knows that Miss Eye is your *ku`uipo*. Did I pronounce that right?"

"I ain't seen Miss Eye, Seth. I suspect she's gone for good."

"But you're still coming here?"

"Sure." He stroked his belly. "I've gotten used to the food. And I like to make sure Checker Cab ain't running the place into the ground."

"Why would you care about that?"

"Because if this places closes, then where am I gonna go?"

"What's up, Seth?" said King from his table.

I couldn't remember the last time George had said hello to me. "What's up, George?"

"Got a question for you. How come you talk to that old fool, but you don't pay no propers to me?"

"I ain't disrespecting you, King," I said. "Stanley Chang and I were just chatting."

"Yeah, well maybe I'd like to do some chatting, too. Why don't you bring your girlfriend over here and sit? At my table." He spread his huge arms wide, as if he were a young lord displaying his kingdom. Maybe that's what he was. I'd never been called to King George's table before, ever, but I nervously pulled Azura over. She squeezed my arm until it hurt. I slid in first and Azura sat on the edge of his booth.

"There you go," said George, without a hint of a smile. "The King ain't so scary. Now who's this girl?"

"I'm Azura." Her voice was quiet but without a shake in it.

"Ah-zoo-rah. What the hell kind of name is that? What's your last name, Ah-zoo-rah?"

"Lear. How old are you?"

George pulled back at the question, and for half a second, he looked young. "Seventeen, last time I checked."

"Then why don't I ever see you in high school?"

"That place, it got nothing to teach me, Ah-zoo-rah Lear."

"Because you know everything? You're a dropout?"

"A dropout? Hell, no. I ain't no dropout. I'm the King." He put his elbows on the table so Azura could see the might of his arms. "Bet you like to mix it up a little bit. You got that look to you. You and me should wrestle a little bit. We could do some damage together. I know that."

Azura blushed. King George smiled. "You thinking about it. I can see you are."

"Knock it off, George," I said.

"Shut your mouth, Seth. I ain't talking to you." His eyes locked on Azura's face, daring her to look away. "So how about it, Ah-zoo-rah Lear?"

She kept blushing, but she held his gaze. "No."

"No? You saying no to the King? You like Seth better? What are you doing hanging out with this orphan trash? This skinny little boy?"

"Seth's not trash. And he's not a boy."

Azura stood up. I joined her. King George shifted his unsmiling eyes to me. "Well, well. So you're a man now, Seth? I knew you were on your own, but I didn't know you were a man. Good to know." He laughed loudly. "Good to know! Hey,

Seth the man, the girl wants to leave. You and your manhood better follow after her. Run along, Seth the man."

I tried not to hurry too obviously as we walked into the kitchen, where Checker Cab was muttering to himself as he mixed up corncake batter. He looked up when we came in. "Damn that King George," Checker muttered quietly. "He sits out there most of the day, making nice folks all uncomfortable. Why's he gotta do that?"

"Who're the two girls, Checker?"

"You mean Shantay and Rachelle? They're my new business plan. My new young waitresses. They'll keep the customers happy while I do the cooking."

"How's that working out so far?"

"They just started today. Come highly recommended from a good buddy of mine, though. Get these girls going and Miss Eye can stay away as long as she likes. I figure if she don't come back, this might just become my restaurant. Might even change the name from Shotgun Shack to Checker's Café."

"Which one's Shantay and which one's Rachelle?"

Checker Cab leaned in toward me with a big grin on his face. "I have no idea. If you find out, let me know." He laughed loudly all by himself.

"You have some information for us, Checker?"

Checker Cab smiled. "I do. Hold on." He peeled off his latex gloves and tossed them in the trash. He led us into the pantry, where floor-to-ceiling shelves held bags of flour and cornmeal, cans of baking powder and salt, and sacks of onions. "I was in here last night, after closing, restocking the shelves by myself, because I ain't got no one to help me. Until today. Hold on a minute." He stopped talking, put his hands behind his hips and arched his back with a groan. "Oh, man. Anyway, I grabbed a can of Clabber Girl off the shelf there and right behind it was…this."

Checker pulled a can of baking soda off the first row, revealing a small bottle made of brown glass. It had a screw-on lid. On the front of the bottle was a white label with black letters. It looked vaguely familiar, but I couldn't think of where I might have seen it before.

"Poison?" I asked.

"You damn right it's poison. Sodium cyanide. Right here among my ingredients. So I asked myself, what kind of fool puts poison in among the ingredients at a restaurant?"

"And what was your answer? And before you say it was Miss Irene, remember that she's the one saved you from—"

"Hold on, Seth. I didn't name any names. And no need for you to talk about how pathetic I was before Miss Irene Dunlop saved me from the gutter. She's gone now. I called you—Seth—I called you because I want to help."

"You called because you want your three hundred dollars."

"Hey, now. I thought you trying to find out who murdered your mother. What was the kind of poison they found in her blood?"

"You know the answer to that."

"It's right here, Seth. Take this down to the police and I'll bet you they'll find this to be a perfect match with what ended your mom's life. And when they do—and when they catch the murderer, whoever she may be—you just remember our little arrangement."

We walked back into the dining room and headed toward the door. "Seth the man," shouted King George, his mouth full of food, "you back to join me at my table? Share a rib-eye with your honey? My treat?"

"No thanks," I said.

"You got something better to do? Where you going?"

"Home."

Nineteen

It was dark when we drove back to the boxing gym. It was closed and the lights were off, which meant ChooChoo wasn't there. Azura and I went through the building and up the stairs toward my apartment. I thought about King George and how he made me feel like a scared little kid, even though he was just a year older than me.

King had left school behind. It seemed he'd left boyhood behind, too, with a wad of cash in his fist. If I decided not to go back to school, would that make me more of a man? I wondered how Mom would have answered that question.

I thought about how easy it was for Checker Cab to drop a dime on Miss Irene after all she'd done for him. I wondered how that poison ended up in the restaurant's kitchen. If it wasn't put there by Miss Irene, who would have put it there? Checker Cab? Would he set up Miss Eye for so little money?

I thought about Azura. She was still with me, even if I'd expected her to bail on me by now. She'd stood her ground with King George better than I had. Maybe she was more than just a rich man's daughter. Maybe she was doing more than just looking for a distraction from the south side of Division Street.

I put my hand on the rusty railing when we reached the bottom of my stairs. We were on the edge of my home. Azura had stairs that led up to her home, too, but hers went from a grassy yard to a sweeping porch. Mine went from a sweaty gym to a tiny apartment.

I wasn't sure I wanted her up there and I wasn't sure why. Was I ashamed of where I lived or was I just protective of it? I missed Mom like crazy right then. I wanted her to open the door and say, "Hey, hon. Who's your friend? Why don't you invite her inside?" Or maybe she'd be passing me on the stairs, on her way to work, and she'd say, "Don't you even think of being alone in our apartment with a girl that pretty."

"Are you going to invite me up?" Azura asked.

"I'm thinking about it."

"What's there to think about?"

"That's what I'm thinking about."

"I can just leave."

"I don't want you to leave."

"Then invite me up."

"I'm not sure I want to do that, either."

We stood there, my hand on the railing, Azura's arms crossed over her chest. I wanted someone else to decide for me. I got my wish when she said, "If it's that hard of a decision, I think I should just go." I walked her silently through the unlit gym. I tried to grab her hand, but she pulled away.

We stepped outside into the darkness of the street. A shadow lunged out from other shadows. Azura let out a scream, which was cut short by a huge hand slapping her on the side of her face. She bounced off the side of the building, her head making a bright crack against the wall, then another when it hit the sidewalk.

"You next, boy," said the shadow. He was massive, whoever he was, dressed in black pants and shirt. A stocking cap and bandana covered nearly all his face. He looked down at me.

"What do you want?" I said, as I prepared to get hit.

"I'm here to deliver a message," he said. His voice was croaky, as if he were intentionally trying to hide his identity. He swung at me. He wasn't fast. I dodged his swing and hit him twice, hard and quick, in his midsection. He was so solid it hurt my hand. He didn't even grunt. I swore.

"I'm here to tell you to lay off." He swung again. I dodged it. I countered again with two more body blows. He didn't even try to block them. He shoved me back with his hands and I fell hard onto my butt.

I scrambled to my feet. "Lay off what?"

"You know what. Get your damn nose out of other people's business."

"My mom was murdered. I'm pretty sure that makes it my business."

"Bad choice," he said. He reached out his huge hands to grab me. When he did, I hit him as hard as I could on the chin. His head snapped, but came right back into line. His arms reached around me. Before I could slip away, he began to squeeze.

The air hissed out of my mouth until I was gasping for breath. Except I couldn't gasp. I could only open my lips, like a fish tossed up onto a pier. I felt myself turning blue. My ribcage was about to collapse and my spine was about to crack. One arm had been pinned against my side. I felt the bone of my arm break, but it was just another pain in a complete embrace of pain. Even my heart hurt. I wondered if it would pop like a balloon.

I was going to die, as certain as 11:59 turns to midnight. I could only think that I wanted the pain to end—wanted the grip to relax so I could fall dead and painless to the sidewalk.

"Leggo," said a voice at least a million miles away. It was a voice I'd heard before, a couple hundred thousand years ago, back before this crushing grip became my entire world. Suddenly, the body that held me rocked, as if it a truck had jumped the curb and smashed into it. The grip remained. The body rocked again, even harder than before. This time the arms loosened. I slipped out and collapsed to the comfort of hard concrete.

"The hell you doin', old man?" asked the voice. And then I recognized it. It was King George. He'd nearly killed me. His huge body was standing over me. Facing this mountain was another mountain—ChooChoo. His arms were loose at his side, but the streetlight shine showed the intent in his eyes. Those eyes looked full of slow-moving blood, more like an ocean tide than a river.

"Y' need to go home, son," said ChooChoo. "This ain't your place."

"You need to mind your business, you washed-up old pug."

"Fine. Y' go on home. I'll mind m' business. We don't want no more trouble."

"You got trouble. I am trouble himself. You know it's true, Old Man. I am young and powerful. You know I can hurt you."

"Lots o' people can hurt me, George. Nothin' special 'bout that."

"You tell that white boy to keep his nose out of my business."

"Boy's just tryin' t' figure out his mom's death. He got a right t' do that."

"His mom wasn't worth the time. Cheap-ass cleaning lady. Half crazy. Busted-up smile. Why bother? Not worth the pain."

ChooChoo barely moved. He just shifted his hips into a diagonal line, but it was enough that I knew an explosion was coming. "Woman meant somethin' t' me, so you best shut your mouth. An' leave."

King George let loose with a couple of sentences full of nasty words. One about ChooChoo and one about my mom. There was nothing for it now. ChooChoo had to lay him down or lay down. That's the law of my neighborhood. A boulder of a fist shot out on the end of ChooChoo's arm and hit King George on the chin, then another quick fist hit him in the gut. ChooChoo's hands moved faster than anyone would have ever guessed as they beat on King George, smashing his face and turning his stomach to bruises.

I'd never seen ChooChoo cut loose and it scared me. I guessed that King George would be dead soon. ChooChoo had committed to the job and he beat George with his hammer hands.

George stumbled back, out of reach. His arms tried to come up into a boxing pose, but he couldn't raise them properly. He looked like a big baby crow with two broken wings, struggling to cross a street. Then one of those broken wings reached inside his jacket and came out with something black and angular. The black thing cracked twice. Short, sharp flares lit up George's bruised and bloody face. His gun hand fell to his side. King George tried to speak—tried to curse, but all that came out of his mouth was a groan. He turned and stumbled up the street.

Dark stains began to spread across the front of ChooChoo's white t-shirt. He looked down at himself, then put one of his big hands over the stains. "You alive, Seth?"

"I think so."

"C'n you call an ambulance?"

I forced my fingers into my pocket and pulled out my phone. I dialed, then told the 911 operator that three of us needed help.

"Tell 'em 'bout the gun," said ChooChoo, as he dropped to his knees. "Makes 'em drive faster."

Twenty

We each rode in our own ambulances—Azura, ChooChoo, and me. By the time I was loaded in mine, my body was shaking uncontrollably and my teeth were chattering. The paramedic—a woman with a square jaw and a man's haircut—covered me in a blanket and told me I was in shock. "Can you tell me what happened?" she asked. My teeth were chattering so hard that I couldn't speak. She pulled my wallet out of my back pocket and looked over my only ID—an ASB card from the high school I hadn't been to in a week. "Is there someone you'd like me to call?" she asked. I tried to come up with a name: Mom was dead. ChooChoo was dying. Azura was riding in her own ambulance, two cars back. And Miss Irene had disappeared. I shook my head no. The paramedic gave me the saddest smile I'd ever seen.

At Tacoma General, the paramedic pulled my gurney out of the ambulance and rolled me into an examination room. A doctor came in and asked me what happened while he shone lights in my eyes and took my blood pressure. I was wheeled into another room, where a skinny, unshaven man with a scar that crinkled his upper lip X-rayed me. I was rolled back into the examination room. Someone jabbed an IV drip into my arm. I grew sleepy, then slept.

I woke up alone in a shared hospital room. My left arm was in a fiberglass cast from the back of my hand to the middle of my bicep. My ribs were wrapped in a bunch of white tape. I was vaguely dressed in a hospital gown and lying under a couple of nubby white blankets. My mouth was dry. My right hand was still connected to an IV drip.

I wanted to call for a nurse to ask for a cup of water, but I knew if one came, I'd ask about ChooChoo and the nurse would tell me he was dead. So I licked my chapped lips with my dry tongue while I stared at the white tiles on the ceiling. I wondered if Azura was in the same hospital and how badly she was hurt. It was my fault. I'd let her come from her safe side of town into my violent life, and she had paid for my selfishness.

I wondered how long I'd been here and where I would go when I left. If I went back home, King George would come after me and finish the job. He'd have to, unless he was going to leave town for good.

My head slowly cleared. I found the controls to the bed and sat myself up. A nurse came in—a midsized, middle-aged woman named Janey with a matter-of-fact look on her face. Nurse Janey asked if I'd like a drink of water. I nodded. Was I hungry? I nodded again.

After I sipped a bit of water from a straw, I managed to croak out enough words to ask Janey what time and what day it was. She told me the date then said it was 11 a.m. I'd only been in the hospital overnight.

"Do you want to know about your friends? Were they your friends?" I nodded my answer to both questions. "I'm not supposed to tell you, but—the girl—Azura? She has a severe concussion and a broken cheekbone, but it appears she'll be okay. If you're feeling better in a while, you can go visit her." Janey set my water cup on a tray next to my head, the straw pointing in my direction, and cleared her throat. "The man— Ernest Baldwin—he's doing less well."

It took my brain a few seconds to realize that Ernest Baldwin must be ChooChoo's real name. I'd never heard it before and never considered that he'd have a name other than the one I'd always called him.

"He's alive then?"

"He is. He has a punctured lung and lost a great deal of blood. He's still in our critical care unit and not taking visitors."

"Is he going to—I mean—will he—is he going to make it?"

"It's too early to tell. I probably shouldn't be sharing this information with you. You'll have to ask his doctor if you want to know more. Sorry." She put her hands on her hips and frowned at me. "Whatever the three of you ran into—I don't know. Bad news. Now you try to relax and I'm going to go find you something to eat."

I turned on the TV to hear voices other than the ones in my head.

Nurse Janey returned with a tray of hospital food. I ate every bit of it—a mysterious piece of meat, vanilla pudding, and a pretty decent rice dish. While I was scraping out the pudding bowl with my spoon, Carlyle walked in.

"I should be saying I told you so, but I'm going to resist."

"So kind of you, Carlyle."

"What happened? And don't BS me. I'll know if you're lying."

"I barely know what happened. I was with a girl—"

"Who?"

"Azura Lear."

"And you know her how?"

"I met her while picking up a clock for Nadel. But she goes to my high school."

"The one you've been skipping?"

"Whatever. I was walking her out to her car in front of ChooChoo's gym when this big guy jumped us."

"You recognize him?"

I should have told Carlyle it was King George. But I didn't. Part of me still didn't trust Carlyle, because he was a cop. Part of me thought that if the cops picked up George, I'd never find out what happened to my mom. I said, "He had a ski mask on. He sent Azura flying and probably would have killed me if ChooChoo hadn't shown up." I went on to tell Carlyle how ChooChoo fought the guy off and how ChooChoo ended up getting shot.

When I finished, Carlyle said, "Are you saying you don't think any of this is connected to your mom's murder?"

"No. I think it *is* connected. And I think it's proof that Miss Irene is innocent."

Carlyle shook his head at me, told me to go back to school, and left. Nurse Janey came back, disconnected me from my IV, and said I could walk around if I wanted to. I asked where Azura's room was. It was only four doors away from mine. I raised myself slowly out of bed and walked across my room on unsteady feet. Without smiling, Janey said I might want to close the back of my hospital gown before I visited any girls. She handed me a robe to wear. It was made of the same white, nubby material as the blankets on the bed. Hospitals must get a bulk discount on that nubby material. I wrapped the robe around me and headed toward Azura's room. I knocked. A male voice said, "Come in." I opened the door.

Azura's father looked at me, his sleepy eyes briefly opening wide, then narrowing into cold slits. He stood, squaring off against me like Kobe Bryant against a Boston Celtic. He had a pretty good stance. I bet he was a ballplayer in his prep school days. I almost smiled.

"You will not come in here," he said, spitting out the words like pieces of bad meat.

"I get it." And I did. If I were him, I wouldn't want me there, either. I practically got his daughter killed. I realized then that he'd been right all along. I was bad for Azura. His sending high school thugs my way to beat me up and chase me off—that was protection for what mattered to him. Maybe it was even love. "I just wanted to see how she was doing," I said.

"It's none of your damn business how she's doing. Just leave her alone."

I could see Azura in the far end of her room, lying asleep or unconscious on the hospital bed. Her head was wrapped in all sorts of bandages, her dark hair spilling out against the white cloth. A tube went in her nose. Another in her arm. Her only sign of life was the slow, slight rise and fall of her chest. I looked silently at her wounded form, then nodded and left.

Twenty-one

I checked out a few hours later and walked unsteadily for the five blocks that separated the hospital from ChooChoo's gym. I grabbed some clothes and picked up Mom's jeep. I drove the Jeep to Shotgun Shack, where I slowly circled the block to see if King George's black BMX bike was out front. When I didn't see it, I parked and went inside.

It was lunchtime and busy, but the only diner I recognized was Stanley Chang—exactly the person I wanted to see. I sat myself in his booth without asking.

"'Sup Stanley?"

"Hey, Seth. Good to see you, little brother. What happened to your arm?"

"King George broke it. He's gonna kill me if he can find me. I need a place to stay, Stanley, and I want to crash at your house."

Stanley stared at me, his mouth open. He finally closed it, then said, "Oh. Wow. Man, I'd love to help you, Seth, but see, my house is being fumigated right now."

"Fumigated, my ass, Stanley. I know Miss Irene is staying with you. Either you let me stay there, too, or I'm turning you both in to the cops."

Stanley glanced around the restaurant, his eyes wide. "What are you trying to do, Seth?"

"I'm trying to stay alive, cuz. So whaddaya say?"

Stanley put down a twenty and we hurried out the door. We jumped in the Jeep and I drove according to his directions. I was growing tired by then and even that short drive was a struggle. He made me park a few blocks away and we walked to his house, a little red bungalow with a half dozen broken-down cars hiding among the weeds in his front yard. He knocked on the door then turned a key in the lock. He stuck his head in and said, "It's me," then pulled me inside and shut the door quickly behind us.

The inside of the house was all shadows. The lights were off. Closed blinds let in a few horizontal cracks of day. A swinging door opened from what must have been the kitchen, because food smells came out of it along with a warm, yellow glow.

Miss Irene stepped from the light and joined me in the shadows.

Twenty-two

"Seth? Is that really you?" Miss Irene rushed forward and wrapped me up in her arms. I groaned when she hugged me. She pulled back and looked at me. "You're hurt. Slugger, what happened to you?"

"King George happened to me, Miss Eye." Miss Irene squinted one eye closed and stared at me from the other, then turned her gaze on Stanley.

"I don't know nothing about it," said Stanley. "Seth said he'd go to the cops if I didn't bring him here."

"That true, Seth?"

"It is. Two things, Miss Eye: One, I need a place to hide from King George. I'm in his crosshairs. He already tried to kill me once and he nearly killed ChooChoo."

"Oh, Lord."

"And two, you need to tell me what the hell you had to do with my mom's murder."

"So it *was* murder?"

"You saying you didn't know?"

"I wasn't sure."

"That's a strange thing for the prime suspect to say."

"Seth, I loved her like my own sister. Maybe more. That's why I couldn't stay away from her funeral. I would never do a thing to harm your mom. "

"Then why'd you run?"

"I'm not proud of it. I ran because of nothing about your mom. I ran because of me—of my past. Stanley, get Seth an iced tea. You want a sandwich or something? This story's gonna take a while."

I followed Miss Irene into the kitchen and sat down heavily on a rickety stool. She pulled out of loaf of brown, unsliced bread, a pink ham, a head of lettuce, a block of cheddar cheese, and jars of mayonnaise and mustard. While she started slicing and spreading, she began telling me about growing up in Spokane and about a young girl named Eve who lived across the street from her.

"She was ten years younger than me, but we were still friends, you know? In that big sister-little sister sort of way. I taught her how to do her hair and wear makeup without putting too much on. She *loved* getting pretty. And she was something to look at, from the day I first met her to the day she died. But when she was a teenager, oh Lord. She was a piece of candy. Boys and men just about couldn't help themselves around her." Miss Irene cut my sandwich along the diagonal and set it on a brown pottery plate. She handed it to me and wiped the mustard off her knife with a wet rag.

"I grew up and went to community college. Worked my way through school as a fry cook at a handful of Spokane restaurants. Took a bunch of accounting classes and got a job at a big real estate office, swearing to myself I'd never work in a restaurant again. Accounts receivable and accounts payable. Nice office and I didn't have to work a fryer, but the pay was lousy. I was still there in my late twenties and still living with my mom, because I couldn't afford to move out." She stopped talking and glared at me. "You gonna eat that sandwich? If you are, I'll make myself one. But if you're just gonna let it sit there, I'll eat it."

I took a bite of my sandwich. It was good. Basic food done right was Miss Irene's specialty.

Miss Irene continued: "It was about then that your mom ran away from home. Her mother—your grandma, I guess—came over a few days later to see if I'd heard from Eve. I lied and said I hadn't, even though she'd already called me two or three times from Tacoma. She was there with a boy—a college student she'd met over the summer. She followed him back to his college in Tacoma and was staying with him in his apartment. Maybe I should have told her parents, but Eve seemed happy and I thought she'd come home in a few days. She didn't. She eventually called her parents to tell them she was staying in Tacoma for good.

"Honestly, I was jealous of your mom. She went independent while she was still in high school. Probably a bad move, but definitely a brave one. Meanwhile, I was twenty-seven and still sleeping every night in my childhood bedroom. Maybe that's part of why I did what I did."

Miss Irene paused and stared across the kitchen at nothing. I looked at her face. Her brown skin was clean and smooth. Her hair was pulled back—mostly black with a few light streaks of gray. Her brown eyes had a sad shine to them.

"Spokane was in the middle of a real estate boom about then, and that real estate office was making all sorts of money. Buying houses at auction for cash, then selling them for twice the amount. Meanwhile, the owner, John J. Jarvis, was still paying me jack. But then he started getting real friendly with me. Giving me hugs. Standing behind me while I worked with his hands on my shoulders. He started hinting to me that he'd pay me more if I'd—you know—be his girlfriend and such. Honestly, it could have been so nice, except he was married. Wife, kids, and that whole perfect thing.

"I guess I was stupid. I thought maybe he loved me. But he just wanted whatever he could get. He sure got me, at least for a time. Then I became pregnant. Believe me, it sure wasn't part of my plan. But I guess I still thought maybe that would change things. All it did was freak him out. He offered to pay me off. Two thousand dollars if I'd leave town and keep the baby to myself. Two thousand. I thought my heart would break. I was so sad and so mad and so damn dumb for ever thinking there was a chance. I almost drove to his house and told his wife the whole thing. But then the baby—my baby boy—died. Never even got born. Never heard him cry."

Miss Eye looked at me and smiled. Sometimes people smile at the strangest times. She wiped a tear from her cheek and then dried her finger on the hem of her dress.

"I told John what had happened. I was so sad, but he was just relieved. He told me how lucky we were and how it meant we could go back to the way things were before. And that did it for me. The next day, I set up a separate bank account for his business, but with my name as primary. Then I transferred all the available money from Mr. John J. Jarvis' business account—almost ninety thousand dollars—into that new account—the one with my name on it.

"That was on a Monday. On Friday, I withdrew all that money in cash. Sometimes we used cash at auctions, so the bank people never blinked. Then I packed up a small overnight bag and told my mom I was spending the weekend with a girlfriend. I got in my car and drove out of town before John came after me. Or before the police did. I've only talked to

Mom a couple of times since then, afraid I'd get caught. Part of the price I paid.

"I went straight to Tacoma. Eve was one of the few people I knew outside of Spokane and she'd been telling me for the last couple of years how much she liked it here. So I came over, me with no baby. Her with you. First thing Eve did was cut my hair real short, like it is now. I used to have the most lovely hair, but I've still never grown it back. Your mom knew some shady characters who helped me get a fake ID, which I used to rent an apartment. The name on the fake ID was Irene Dunlop. I didn't even choose the name, but I kind of liked it.

"What was your name before?"

"Wanda Knight." Miss Eye stared across the room again, then repeated the name. "Wanda Knight. I haven't said that out loud in at least ten years. It was a nice name. When I was a little girl, I used to pretend I'd grow up to be a famous singer. I'd stage awful little shows for my mom and she would introduce me as 'The Wanderful Wanda Knight.' Anyway, I took a job at Shotgun Shack as a cook—for the old owner, whose name was Edna Jenkins. It was a crummy little restaurant in those days."

I asked, "Why'd you work if you had all that money?"

"It scared me. I thought I should wait a while. When I started working here, the food was lousy, the dining room was lousy, the service was lousy. But being back in that kitchen was a good place for me to hide. On my breaks, I'd go down to the library to read the Spokane newspaper to see if there was any mention of me. As far as I could tell, I never made the news. But one day a few months later, when I phoned my old house, my mom said the police had come by looking for me."

"They put a warrant out for your arrest?"

"I didn't know then and I still don't know. How would I find that out without getting caught? Anyway, Edna was barely making enough in those days to keep herself in flour and sugar. One night, while we were closing up, she told me she was probably gonna shut the place down. On a whim, I asked her what she'd take for it. She sold me the name, the sign, and all the equipment for fifteen thousand, plus taking over another seventeen thou in debt. I paid her thirty-two thousand dollars in twenties. She didn't blink. The ownership was transferred to my new name. And I've been here ever since, running this place as Irene Dunlop. The only one in all of Tacoma who knew different was your mom."

I wondered if my mom was mad enough at Miss Irene to threaten to expose her. I wondered if keeping that secret meant enough to Miss Irene that she killed Mom to keep it quiet. My thoughts must have showed on my face, because Miss Irene said, "I didn't kill your mom, Slugger. I loved her, you know. She was all the family I really had anymore. Her and you. And that fool, Checker."

"Then why'd you run?"

"Because that cop came around. He started asking questions. I knew if he asked enough, he'd connect me back to Spokane, back to my crime there. I'd end up in jail. I'd lose the restaurant and my life here. Everything."

"Why didn't you just repay the money?"

"Because I deserved it. It was mine. I'll never give that man a dime, Seth. But I've been paying it back, in my own way." She stared at me as she spoke. It was a stare that meant I was supposed to understand something, but I didn't get it.

I shrugged. "What happens next? You just keep hiding and let Checker Cab run your restaurant into the ground?"

"That dumb S.O.B.? He better not screw things up, or I'll come after him with a carving knife."

I laughed. "He's actually doing a half-decent job. Biscuits aren't as good, but he's hired a couple of hot young girls to help him out in the dining room."

"He did *what*? Stanley didn't say anything about that."

"Least he's keeping the place open."

"Yeah, and robbing me blind in the process."

I gave Miss Eye a sideways look. She rolled her eyes. "I suppose you think I can't complain about that, hmm?"

I shrugged.

Miss Irene continued with another sad smile. "Checker's all right, Seth. He'll come through okay. Least I hope he will. Besides, I ain't really got a plan, Slugger. Guess I trust the cops to figure it out. All I know is I didn't do it."

"Cops move pretty slow. How long you willing to wait?"

Miss Eye said nothing, but her shiny brown eyes got even shinier.

I said, "It's a good story. But there's one thing that makes no sense. How come you wouldn't pay to fix Mom's tooth?"

Miss Irene pushed some of my sandwich crumbs around the tabletop. She spoke without looking up. "I did pay. Eleven hundred dollars out of my own pocket. I gave it to Eve in cash, which is what she asked for. Probably a mistake. I don't know where that money went, Seth, but I gave it to her the same month that she broke her tooth. After a few months, she started claiming I never paid her. We argued about that for a while, then I just thought, 'Screw it. I'll pay again.' So I agreed to. All she had to do was go to the dentist and send me the bill. But she wanted cash again. I refused. She said I didn't trust her. I didn't. I loved her, but I didn't trust her."

"Me neither."

"I told her I thought she blew her tooth money getting high."

"She probably did."

"That's what we were fighting about on that last night."

She looked up. I looked down. I suddenly realized how tired I was. My painkillers were wearing off. I wanted to take a couple more, then fall asleep. I said so. Miss Irene led me to a spare bedroom, where she had to clear a half-dozen cardboard boxes off an unmade bed. She offered to make it with clean sheets, but I didn't want to wait. She threw a blanket down on the bare mattress. I threw myself on top of it. Miss Irene threw another blanket on top and I was out.

Twenty-three

I slept until the next afternoon. I went into the kitchen, brewed some coffee, then tried calling the hospital to check on ChooChoo and Azura, but the floor nurse wouldn't tell me about either one if I wasn't a relative. I decided to go and see for myself, even though Miss Irene tried to talk me out of it.

Stanley gave me the keys to the mostly-yellow Chevy pickup in his front yard. Its front bumper was held on with electrical wire and the only door that opened was the passenger side, but it started on the first turn. The radio didn't work, so I drove in silence. I parked in the hospital garage to stay off the street and walked across a sky bridge to the lobby. I went to see ChooChoo first. He was awake, meaning that one eye was half open. He still had tubes in his arm and nose, and another tube taped to his chest, but his wide lips twitched in the direction of a smile when he saw me. "Hey, boy," he whispered. "Nice to know you alive. Last time I saw you, you was a pile on the sidewalk."

"Same with you," I said. "What's the prognosis?"

"Prognosis is it gon' take more 'n a young thug like King George to kill this ol' man."

"That's good to know. How much longer they gonna keep you in here?"

"Be a while, it sounds like. My lung's gotta heal up a bit." ChooChoo coughed weakly for about fifteen seconds, then said, "The first thing 'm gonna do is spar with you. So you better heal up quick, 'cause you owe me a chance to whup your butt."

This was love talk for ChooChoo. This was how he told me he loved me like a son.

"You try it, old man. With one more lung than you, I might be the one doing the whupping."

"Yeah. You with one arm an' me with one lung."

"Hey Chooch, what were you doing at the gym that late, anyway?"

"Coffee."

"Huh?"

"Couldn't sleep. Was thinkin' 'bout yo' mom. Then thought 'bout you. Then I wanted a cuppa coffee. Just had t' have one. So I drove to the gym to see if there was any left in the pot. Guess your coffee saved your life. Seth, why you wanna keep after this mess? Maybe let the police handle it. Maybe they right 'bout Miss Eye."

"They're not. I've seen her. Now I need to prove it. And it's your fault that I do."

"You ain't makin' sense, son."

"Sure I am. You're the one told me to get a family. You said if I didn't you'd make me move out. Other than you, Miss Eye is the closest thing to family I got."

ChooChoo nodded at me, as if I'd just said the most obvious thing in the world. I said: "You on real food yet?"

"If you c'n call this real food. Maybe you could bring me a Frisko Freeze burger an' a butterscotch shake."

"I'll bring it back by today, Chooch. Get a little good Frisko Freeze grease into you and you'll be back in the ring in no time."

He nodded. "Been layin' here thinkin' an' there's somethin' else I need ya t' do." He coughed. I waited. Then he said: "There's a picture on m' desk of your mom an' me. Inside it, behind the photo, is a key to m' bottom desk drawer. Open that drawer. You'll see some envelopes there. Bring 'em back here and you 'n me 'll have a talk. 'Bout your mom."

I left him to his nurses. But hearing ChooChoo's voice—even in a whisper—was like taking a deep breath for me. I filled my lungs on it one more time, then walked down the hall toward Azura's room, keeping an eye peeled for her father or any of his watchdogs.

I opened the door and looked inside. Erik Jorgenson was there, sitting next to Azura's bed. I expected him to chase me away, but he just stared at me for five seconds, then nodded. I approached.

"You standing guard?" I asked.

"Something like that." No one spoke for a while, then Erik said, "You want something?"

"Just to see how she is."

"She'll live. She goes home later today. I'm surprised you care."

"Really? You think I don't care about her?"

"If you did, you wouldn't have let this happen."

Maybe Erik was right. I had to think about it and my post-beating mind still wasn't working very well. I stared at this kid, wondering if he was what Azura needed. His hair was freshly cut and had that healthy sheen of a good diet. His skin was dermatologist-smooth. He wore an Adidas track suit, unzipped so I could see his Patagonia t-shirt underneath and a heavy gold chain. His shoes were LeBrons, almost the same as mine, but that was about the only thing similar about us. His clothes and looks said money, but more than that, they said safety. I wondered how much safety was worth. More than love? Looking at Azura, sleeping under bandages, I wasn't sure.

I thought about the arguments I could make. Azura sought me out, right? I didn't encourage her, did I? And boys and girls in my neighborhood had a right to love whoever they wanted, didn't they?

"I'll leave now," I said, "if you'll do one thing for me."

"You making demands? Seriously?"

"It's a small one, and it gets me out of here."

"What is it?"

"Just tell her I stopped by."

"If I say I will, how do you know I'll actually do it?"

"Guess I'll just have to trust you."

Erik smirked at me, then shook his head. "You stay," he said, "and I'll go."

It was my turn to smirk.

He said, "Honestly, I don't want to be here when she wakes up, because every time she wakes, the first thing she does is ask about you. I can barely stand it."

I watched Erik leave and wondered if he might be a better man than me. I sat in the chair next to Azura.

Ten minutes later, her eyes opened, reminding me how big and deep they were. She saw me and said, "Hey."

"Hey back atcha. How are you feeling?"

"Sleepy. Happy. To see you, I mean. Where have you been?"

"In an adjustable bed of my own. And Dad wasn't all that keen on letting me inside your room."

"You came by?"

"I did."

"How many times?"

"Once. Plus just now."

"Oh."

"Erik was here. I'm pretty sure he was supposed to keep me away, but he left me with you. The fool."

"Why's he a fool?"

"Because." Then I stopped. I was gonna say something witty, like how I couldn't be trusted around a beautiful girl like her and then I was going to kiss her. Instead, I closed my eyes and tried to imagine a life without her. I could do it, just barely. "Azura, I'm working to figure this whole thing out. I mean, your dad and your boyfriend and all that."

"Erik is not my boyfriend. He thinks he owns me."

"Yes. But he thinks he loves you. He's the one who stayed here."

"My dad probably paid him to."

"It doesn't look like he needs the money. And if your dad paid him, it's because your dad is trying to protect you—"

"My dad—"

"—and by the looks of things, you need protecting."

"I hope this isn't your way of saying get well soon, because it's not making me feel better."

"Here's the deal," I said. "I'm still in the middle of this thing. This mess of my life. But I'm gonna see it through. When it's over, I'll come see you. I promise. But before then, I'm gonna disappear for a bit. Don't try to find me, because I couldn't live with myself if something worse happened to you."

She said a few words about me tossing her aside, but I didn't stick around to listen. I went outside. Erik was out there waiting, like I hoped he would be. No fond farewells were exchanged.

Twenty-four

I sat inside Stanley's yellow pickup and called Shotgun Shack on my cell phone. After the twentieth ring, someone finally picked up. I could hear Checker Cab yelling from the background, "Do I have to answer the damn phone myself? Does anyone else even work here?" Then a young female voice bitterly said, "Shotgun Shack. Shantay speaking. May I help you?" It sounded like helping me was the last thing Shantay wanted to do.

"Let me talk to Checker," I said.

"Better you than me."

A few minutes of hold time later, Checker finally came on. "Whoever it is, you got thirty seconds."

"Checker, it's Seth. I'll make it quick."

"Good, 'cause it's busy *and it seems I'm the only one working tonight.*" He shouted the end of that sentence to the room.

"King George been in there lately?"

"He just left. He came by asking about you. Didn't buy a thing."

"What'd you tell him?"

"The truth. That I ain't seen or heard from you in days. Where you at, son?"

I wasn't about to tell Checker. He meant me no harm, but a few hundred-dollar bills or a King George clenched fist just might make him talk too much. "George say where he was going when he left?"

"Naw. He rode his bike west on Sixth, though. But I ain't no dating service. Next time you call during a dinner rush, you better have a food order, cash money you wanna give me, or at least news about Miss Irene coming back."

"You want her back?"

"Oh, please. Get that woman back here. I can't take much more of this."

"What about your new business plan? Shantay and Rachelle?"

"Damn. You know how it is, Seth. The better looking they are, the less work they're willing to do. Just get me Miss Eye."

"I'll do my best, Checker. But you know Miss Irene seems to have disappeared off the face of the planet."

"Then I'm screwed."

My broken arm itched. I stuck a finger as far down inside the cast as I could, but I couldn't reach the itch. I said, "Here's the deal, Checker: I might be able to get Miss Irene back. Problem is, I'm not all that inclined to help you, because I'm probably gonna end up owing you three hundred dollars for finding that jar of poison."

"You mean for my information leading to the whereabouts? What if you didn't have to pay me the full amount?"

"How much of a discount are we talking?"

"A hundred dollars?"

"Checker Cab," I said, "I won't even get out of bed for less than two hundred."

The other end of the phone was silent. Then Checker said, "Just bring her back, Seth. Bring her back and we'll forget the whole thing."

I drove Stanley's yellow pickup past Shotgun Shack and continued west along Sixth Avenue, keeping my eye out for King George, wondering what the heck I would do if I saw him.

Then I found his bike. Or it found me. George pedaled it out of a driveway and glided past the front fender of Stanley's pickup. He must not have seen me, as George stared straight ahead as he rode. He cut across Sixth Avenue, dodging cars. I was about to follow him when I saw that he'd turned out from Nadel's House of Clocks. I pulled to the curb.

The car parked in front of me was Nadel's—his baby blue forty-year-old Cadillac El Dorado that looked nearly new. The lights were on in Nadel's shop, but the *closed* sign was on the door. I knocked. No answer. I went around to the back and knocked on the workshop's alley door. Still nothing. Mom's ring of client keys was still in my pocket. I pulled it out and tried them until one fit in Nadel's workshop door. I stepped inside.

A tiny spring crunched under my foot. The floor of the usually neat shop was covered in springs and gears, as if a clock had come undone in midair. Lying among the loose parts was Nadel, his head bent at a strange angle, his eyes open and staring at the ceiling. He was dead.

The shop was turned inside out. Drawers were pulled out. Cupboards were emptied. Parts were scattered across countertops and all over the floor.

I decided it was time to call Carlyle and started punching his number in my phone. Before I hit the call button, I saw two books lying next to Nadel on the floor. I'd seen those books recently in his shop. Now they were lying next to Nadel's dead body. I picked them up and carried them out to Stanley's truck, then went back inside. There was one other thing I wanted to see before the police arrived.

I found Nadel's stepstool and brought it over to his workbench. I climbed the stool and opened the cabinet above the workbench. Usually, the top shelf held an orderly row of cans and jars of the chemicals Nadel used for the gold and silver plating of old, worn clock parts. This time, the cupboard was a scattered mess. I studied the contents of the shelf for a minute, then went out front and called Carlyle.

He showed up within five minutes, along with an ambulance and about a half-dozen uniformed cops. If you want great service from the police department, someone just has to die.

Carlyle grunted at me when he arrived at the scene, then went to the front door. It was locked. "How'd you get in?"

"The back door was open," I lied.

"Wait for me right here." Carlyle and his wake of cops went around to the back. The two uniforms directly behind him had their pistols drawn.

He returned ten minutes later, looking even more tired than when he'd gone in. "I suppose you think this is related to your mom somehow."

"I do. The guy who did this is the same guy who almost killed Azura, ChooChoo, and me. I saw him ride away from here right before I called."

"And that would be King George?"

"How'd you know that?"

"Your friend ChooChoo gave us his name in the hospital. Unlike you. Real name is George Carson. Bad news. Used to drive around a big Lincoln SUV. Now he rides around on a kid's bike. How you know him?"

"Known him half my life. Used to go to school together. Least when he wasn't in jail. He hangs out at Shotgun Shack and terrorizes customers."

"Why'd he try to kill you?"

"Because I was snooping around about Mom's murder."

"If you knew he was the one who nearly killed you, why didn't you tell me when I asked earlier?"

I shrugged.

"And now another innocent man's dead."

"Maybe not innocent."

"Meaning?"

"I think maybe Nadel killed my mom."

"What makes you think that?"

"A couple of things. First of all, I saw Nadel and King George eating together at Shotgun Shack after mom died."

"So?"

"Nadel eats vegetarian. Even the cornbread at Shotgun Shack has pig fat in it. And the only people who ever sit with King George are other thugs and girls who are stupid enough to think George might give them a little of his money."

"You think Nadel killed your mom, then went to one of your favorite hangouts to hire some protection? Is he really that stupid?"

"Shotgun Shack is like King George's office. If you want George, that's where you have to go. And maybe Nadel didn't know I hung out there."

"You're saying he didn't know?"

"I'm saying I doubt he would. Nadel wasn't interested in much other than clocks and money."

"What'd Nadel and George talk about?"

"How should I know? But I bet it had something to do with my mom."

"I knew you'd say that."

"Azura and I went to pick up a clock at Nadel's. He seemed really nervous when he saw me. And after he thought Azura and I had left, he called someone to tell them that I was there.

That was the same day that King George practically beat us to death."

"Nadel and your mom get along?"

"Like family. One of her oldest customers. I practically grew up in his shop."

"But you still think he killed her?"

"You saying family members never kill each other?"

Carlyle rubbed his eyes with the palms of his hands. "No. I'm not saying that."

I thought about that old man lying broken on his workshop floor. Nadel and I had history together—thousands of hours in his workshop. Was it really that easy for him to kill my mom? What was worth more to him than her life?

Carlyle spoke. "Nadel died of a broken neck and blows to the head. He was beaten to death. He was a small man, but it's harder to kill someone that way than most people think. Whoever did it was big and strong. For now, King George is our primary suspect. I'll radio in his information now, but you better be playing straight with me."

"I am."

Carlyle sighed. "I'm sure you have a theory on why Nadel would have killed your mother."

"I don't, but there's one other thing I want to show you." Carlyle followed me inside. I told him to look in the cabinet above the workbench. Carlyle sighed again and climbed the stepstool. He stared inside the cabinet for a few seconds, then said, "How long have you known this was here?"

"I just found it tonight, but I should have figured it out sooner. Cyanide is one of the chemicals used in metal plating. Nadel's had it here for years."

Carlyle reached in and pulled out a small brown bottle with

a white label that read *sodium cyanide*. It was identical to the bottle Checker Cab found at Shotgun Shack.

"Is there anything else you know that you're keeping from me?"

I thought about the books I'd put in the truck, but said, "No."

"Go home, Seth. Leave this work to us now, okay?"

I left without answering, but wasn't about to go home. If King George was riding around tying up loose ends, I didn't want him to find me.

Instead I drove to King's Books. The store was closed, but Sweet Pea was still inside, sorting stacks of used paperbacks. He let me in, where the smell of dust and old paper made my nose wrinkle.

I set the books down on the counter. One was *A Detailed Account of the Battle of Yorktown by an Attendant Soldier,* by Captain Elliot Black. The other, *Private Affairs of George Washington, from the Records and Accounts of Tobias Lear, Esquire, His Secretary* by Stephen Decatur Jr. As Sweet Pea picked them up he said, "These seem pretty rare. You looking for cash or credit?"

"Neither. I'm looking for Mom's murderer. And I think these books might help me."

"How?"

"I was hoping you could tell me. Any obvious connections between these two books?"

"Sure. The Battle of Yorktown was the most famous battle led by George Washington. Turning point of the Revolutionary War and all that. And Tobias Lear was George Washington's secretary. That the kind of connection you're talking about?"

"Not what I was thinking. Any of this connected to anyone in Tacoma?"

"No. This is all East Coast stuff. Snooty old rich families who trace their lineage back to the *Mayflower*. That sort of nonsense. You don't get much of that here, which is one of the reasons we all love Tacoma so."

The name Lear seemed too much of a coincidence. "What about Lear?"

"What about him?"

"You think this Tobias could be connected to the Lears who live around here?"

"You mean the investment guy? The rich one?"

"That's the one." I told Sweet Pea about Azura and her family—how I'd gone to the Lear house to pick up an antique clock the day before my mom was murdered. Sweet Pea listened while his eyes scanned the spines of the books in his store, as if he was cataloging my conversation in its proper place.

When I finished, he said, "Let me tell you what I know. Tobias Lear was a real rascal. George Washington hired him to run his private affairs. Lear was once caught collecting rent from one of Washington's tenants and putting the money in his own pocket. When Washington died, Lear had possession of all of Washington's papers. When other founding fathers asked for them, Lear handed over a very incomplete collection. In fact, he destroyed whole sections of Washington's personal diary. Some say it was to save key government leaders from the embarrassment of scandal. Because you know those old boys had a few scandals. Chopping down cherry trees was just the beginning."

"What's that have to do with the Battle of Yorktown?"

"I give up. What?"

"You don't know?"

"No. You want me to do some research?"

"Would you?"

"I should make you do it, you slacker. Why aren't you in school?"

"I'm trying to decide if I want to go back. If it's worth it."

"Of course it's not worth it. But you do it because you have to. Every now and then you just have to suck it up and play by the rules. That's the only way to get your union card."

"Kind of blows, though."

"High school is supposed to be hell. You're supposed to be miserable during it. That's how it's designed."

It was nine o'clock. I was tired again. I drove to Frisko Freeze to pick up some dinner for ChooChoo and me. Two cheeseburgers. Two fries. Two butterscotch shakes. Frisko Freeze is famous for being delicious but slow, so while I waited, I kept a close eye out for King George's bike. That got me paying attention to cars—and the people inside of them. It made me realize how not-happy people look most of the time. Not sad, necessarily. Just not happy. Most drivers were either hunched over their wheels or slumped back in their seats, looking sleepy, bored, or mildly disgusted with where they were going. Not all. A blue Subaru wagon full of teenagers pulled into the Frisko Freeze lot. Their windows were rolled down and the music was blaring. Three boys and two girls were singing along with a song I didn't recognize. They were high school kids and they'd figured out how not to be miserable.

When my order came, I consoled my lonely soul with grease.

I drove back toward the hospital to deliver ChooChoo's dinner, then remembered his request to pick up the envelopes from his office. I changed my route and parked in front of the gym.

The photo of ChooChoo and Mom stared at me from the top of ChooChoo's messy desk. I picked it up and pried the cardboard off the back. A small brass key fell out. I fit it into a keyhole on his bottom desk drawer. The drawer was full of receipts and bank statements. I dug through those until I came upon a box of envelopes. I picked it up and opened it.

The envelopes inside were blue—the same color as the envelopes I'd received once a month, from my absent father, for as long as I could remember.

I drove in a fog back to the hospital, trying to make sense of the box lying on the seat next to me. ChooChoo was asleep when I arrived, but I shook his shoulder roughly and told him to wake up. He opened his eyes, then sat up with only the slightest groan, his eyes locking on the box of blue envelopes in my hand. I set his food on his tray, but he didn't touch it.

He struggled to sit up. "Not sure if you'll think this is good news or not."

"So you've been the one sending the checks to me?"

"Me? No." He held out his big hand. I put the envelopes in them. "Y' mom asked me to keep these for her. Once a month she'd come 'n get one from me. Just did it again a week or so ago." He paused to catch his breath, while his thick fingers pulled a single envelope from the box.

I stood next to the bed, not saying a word.

"You wanna set down?" said ChooChoo.

"No."

"You sure?"

"Just tell me."

"Your dad ain't never sent you anything, Seth. An' I'm sorry 'bout that. It was your mom the whole time, ev'ry time."

"What the hell." It wasn't a question.

"Thought you should know."

"It doesn't make any sense."

"Did to her. She wanted you t' think your dad cared 'bout you. So she'd set aside some money and write you the little notes each month—"

"I've always hated those notes."

"Wasn't easy for her to keep that money aside. Sometimes she had t' borrow it from me. Lots of times Miss Eye paid."

I nodded, thinking back to Miss Eye's comment about paying back the money she stole. "Did everyone know about this but me?"

"Just us three. Each month she'd send these envelopes inside another letter to a couple of her friends in some far-off cities."

"Let me guess. St. Louis. And Pensacola and Taos, New Mexico."

"Might be. She'd ask 'em to mail 'em back to you. She thought you might be a bit more forgivin' of your father if you thought he was far away."

"What the hell?" I looked at the blue envelope in ChooChoo's hand. "So my dad—"

"She's never heard from him. Never wanted to. But she wanted you—"

"I get it," I lied.

"Thought you should know."

"So you said."

I took the remaining envelopes and left. On the way to Stanley Chang's house, I opened the window of the Jeep and threw them out. Through the rearview mirror, I could see the envelopes fluttering in the air, then sticking to the wet pavement. A car ran over them and they mixed in permanently with the rest of the litter.

The problem with dead parents and with missing parents is that there's no one left to yell at.

Twenty-five

I woke up the next morning to the smell of coffee and biscuits. The smell was the only thing that pulled me out of my backroom bed. I walked into the kitchen, where Miss Irene was washing the dishes. I was still deciding if I was mad at her for her part in the whole envelope thing. She turned around when I came in and passed me a sad smile.

"You hungry?"

"I could eat a little something."

"That's just what your mom always said. You got that part of her. That ungreedy nature."

"You saying I'm like her?"

"I'm saying part of you is. And the rest of you is just Seth."

I pulled a couple of Miss Eye's hot biscuits apart with my fingers as she poured me a cup of coffee and milk. I wiped butter across the insides of the biscuits. She slid the cup my direction and said, "What you gonna do when you find the man who killed your mom?"

"You ask like you think it'll happen."

"Course it will, Slugger. You're one of the smartest people I know."

"How do you know it's a man?"

"Honey, it's always a man. Trust me on that one. Only time it's a woman is when a man drove her to it, so even then it's a man. That's how God made them. Men are born killers."

"Me too?"

She smiled, "When you become a man, I'll let you know."

"Damn. And what are women? Born liars?"

"You're all full of love this morning."

My phone buzzed then. It was a text from Azura.

You still alive?

I texted back. *Still am.*

I miss you. Hope you can come and see me.

I need a few days.

I need to tell you something.

Give me a few more days, I texted. I needed to keep her out of this business until it was over. *Got to focus on this mess and get it behind me.*

My phone stared at me without a response for a while, then buzzed. *Okay, but I really need to talk to you.*

I need to talk to you, too, I texted. I hoped we both meant *need* the same way.

I checked in with Sweet Pea at noon, but the store had been unusually busy that morning and he hadn't found anything yet. He told me to check back around dinnertime. I didn't much feel like driving around in broad daylight while King George and who knew which of his friends were out looking for me, so I spent the afternoon cleaning Stanley's house. I owed Stanley for taking me in and for me bringing more danger into his life.

While I mixed bleach and water and pulled one rubber glove onto my hand that wasn't in a sling, I thought about Mom, about how she'd taken this humble job seriously, night after night, even if she seemed to treat the rest of her life as if it was one big vacation, me included. With one arm, I scrubbed Stanley's kitchen floor and the tubs and toilets in the two bathrooms. I polished chrome faucets and mirrors. I used vinegar and old newspapers to clean the dust and streaks off his windows. I vacuumed his carpets and dusted his crappy, dark-wood furniture. The house was still a dump when I was done, but it was a clean dump, from top to bottom. It smelled sharp.

Sweet Pea finally called me at a few minutes past seven. "I think I've got as much as I can manage to pull together. It's something, but I don't know what it means. You want to come by?"

Fifteen minutes later, I was inside King's Books, where Sweet Pea had both of the old books laid out on a side counter. A half-dozen pages in each volume were marked with yellow Post-it notes.

"So here's the deal: Aside from being a helluva soldier, George Washington was pretty serious about record-keeping. Immediately after the Battle of Yorktown, Washington had two maps of the battle commissioned. Both were hand-drawn by a Frenchman named Jean Baptiste Gouvion. The first one was made as the official record of the battle. But Washington had Gouvion make him another map as well—a smaller one that Washington could carry around in his pocket. Supposedly, Washington liked to pull that map out with his buddies and show them just how amazing a feat the battle was. But after Washington's death, that map disappeared."

"Okay. So that's the Yorktown connection. What's that have to do with Tobias Lear?"

"Like I told you yesterday, Lear was Washington's personal secretary and a real rascal. He had sticky fingers. And when Washington died, quite a bit of Washington's personal documents seemed to have stuck to Tobias Lear's fingers."

"Including the map?"

"That's the theory by plenty of historians. But look. Your girlfriend's last name is Lear. A pretty common name, but there aren't that many Lears with as much money as your Lear has. And guess what else?"

"What?"

"I did a search online for Tobias Lear and found this article." Sweet Pea pointed to his computer screen. The website was called Frobisher's Auction News. The headline of the article said, "Lear-Olmstead estate sets Maine auction record."

"Don't read the whole thing," said Sweet Pea. "Skip down to right…about…here." His finger pointed to the following paragraph:

> *Last December, a barn on the Olmstead estate was sold to one of the family members. The barn contained a large collection of furnishings and documents. Most of the property was auctioned off last Saturday. Notable items that were listed as being distributed to other Olmstead and Lear family members included a collection of silver, a set of personal letters of Tobias Lear, and a pendulum wall clock.*

"I picked up a clock from the Lears' house. Nadel fixed it."

"So you told me. It's got to be the same clock. Too much of a coincidence."

"But you weren't talking about a clock. You were talking about a map."

"Sure. But at least we've made a connection. Your Lears must be connected to the Battle of Yorktown Lear. And that map is mentioned in these last couple sentences. Listen." He read from the website.

"'Notably missing from the auction items was George Washington's personal map of the Battle of Yorktown. Long thought to be in the possession of a Lear family member, the map has never been produced since Washington's death. Were it to surface at auction, it would likely set new records once again.'"

I felt suddenly lightheaded. I grabbed Sweet Pea's counter for support. "I think I've seen that map."

Twenty-six

I was going to head back to Nadel's shop by myself, but Sweet Pea wouldn't let me leave until I called Carlyle. The sleepy cop seemed annoyed and only half-interested, until I told him I was going inside the store whether he was there or not.

"That's breaking and entering, Seth," Carlyle drowsed into the phone. "Felony charge."

"I'm not breaking in. I have a key. See you there."

I parked the truck on a side street and entered the shop through the back door, turning on the workshop light. The workshop was still the same turned-over mess it had been when I'd found Nadel's body. It was a place of metal and wood—not paper. Veneers, gears, springs, wire, pliers, diodes, solenoids, motors, chains, stains, and paint were thrown crazily around the floor. I gave the room a quick onceover, looking for the yellowed, crumpled piece of paper I'd seen for only a few seconds, back when this whole thing began.

I searched for fifteen minutes without finding a thing, then went out into the showroom. In the relative silence of the evening the room was an eerie space of ticks and tocks. *Where would Nadel hide a map, if he hid it here at all?*

The map was originally inside a clock, and now it could be inside any of the hundred or so clocks on the walls and floor. Each one had a cabinet of some sort. But which one would it be? I could start at one end and work my way around the showroom, but that would take all night.

Then I remembered that the map had originally been the reason the Lears' clock hadn't run, so I started scanning the room for a clock whose pendulum wasn't swinging. It took me a minute, but I spotted one—an Americana-styled regulator that looked like it came from a small-town general store about a hundred years ago. Nadel had shown it to me before. It was a beat-up old Hermle. Wasn't worth much, but Nadel had said it was the first clock he'd ever been paid to fix. When he had it running, he offered to buy it from that initial customer. He'd paid only fifty bucks for it, but it had stayed in his shop, ticking and Westminster-chiming ever since. Today, it wasn't ticking. The pendulum hung still.

I was about to lift it from the wall when I heard the back door of the shop open and close.

"I'm in the showroom, Carlyle," I called.

"That you, my man?" It was a deep voice. One I hoped I didn't recognize.

"Who's there?"

"Walt Disney." King George stepped through the shop door and smiled. "Welcome to Disneyland."

"Hey, George," I said, trying to hide the shake in my throat. "I figured I'd see you again one of these days."

"You just can't keep your nose out of other people's business," he said, moving out from behind the counter.

"It is my business," I said. "It was my mom that was murdered." I stayed square with him, just as if I was in a boxing ring. He moved toward me and I circled around the showroom, out of his way. The clocks were ticking in the background.

"I just might kill you, but I didn't kill your mom. Nadel did. You should thank me for avenging you. I should send you a bill."

"So why you want me?" I just needed to keep King George talking until Carlyle arrived and I needed to keep his hands from closing around my neck.

"You in the way. You between me and that map."

"That's what this is about for you, too?"

"It's what it's been about for everyone. That's why your mom's dead."

"That's what I figured." My eyes darted toward the front windows, hoping to see Carlyle's car roll up to the curb. "Nadel took the map out of the Lears' clock, thinking it was a piece of trash. I'm guessing that my mom found the map while she was cleaning. Nadel must have been working late. I can picture my mom teasing him for throwing the map away. Mom would have known the map was valuable. She was no saint, but for something like that, she would have told Nadel they needed to return it."

"That right there's what got her killed," said George.

"Maybe so," I said, "because Nadel loved his money. Even more than I thought. And knowing the map came from inside a Lear family clock—Nadel recognized that it was worth a fortune. He wanted to steal the map and Mom was the only one who could point a finger at him. So he poisoned her with the cyanide he used for gold- and silver-plating—how, I'm not sure—then drove her body back to ChooChoo's and left her in her car. That about right?"

"Not bad, Sherlock. He made her a cup of tea. She didn't need to drink much."

"Cup of tea? She would have loved that. So he actually did it. Snuffed out Mom's life for a piece of old paper."

"I told him he was a dumbass for killing her. He could've given her a share to shut her up—like you said, she was no saint. He said he didn't want to take any chances. But that map—old dude figured it was his free and clear except for your mom.

"She died for no good reason?"

"Reason is that he panicked. People do that when there's a million dollars on the line."

"A million dollars. So that's how much Mom was worth to him."

"You done yet?"

"No. I figure Nadel got nervous when the police questioned him and when I started poking around. So he paid you to throw the blame onto Miss Irene and to chase me off. That's what you two were talking about when I saw you at Shotgun Shack. Then you brought a bottle of Nadel's cyanide and hid it in the pantry at Shotgun Shack, in a place where you knew Checker Cab would find it. And you beat me up to scare me away. Now I'm done."

"Nadel didn't come to me, boy. I came to him. He practically ran me over with your mom's Jeep the night he killed her. Dumb luck that I was there. But I was. I saw him driving your mom's Jeep. And that is what we were talking about at Shotgun Shack. That I knew he killed her. That I wanted to know why he did it. That I wanted payment. But he wouldn't pay me cash. He's too much of a cheap ass."

George flexed the fingers of his hands. "Old man took some convincing. But with a little friendly conversation, he finally told me about the map. With a little more convincing, he told me how much he might get for it. He said he'd pay me five percent—fifty thou if he sold it for a million, which he thought he could get. He's connected. Antiques collectors and all." King George took two slow steps my direction.

"But *you're* not connected—not to those kinds of buyers," I said, dancing away from him. "You don't exactly seem like an antiques kind of guy. And now that you killed Nadel, how are you gonna sell the map?"

"I ain't a fool like you," he said, his voice rumbling even lower. "I made sure that he gave me his connection before I beat the life out of him. Dumb old man thought he could control me, because I'm a kid. But no one controls me. I'm the king."

"So you've said."

King George took a step toward me. I moved back and to my right, still facing him. "What I can't figure is how you can sell it. That map is famous. Soon as the sale becomes public, you get caught."

"Not all sales become public," he said, moving a few inches toward me. "Some people just like to own stuff."

"So now all you got to do is find the map. You didn't find it here last time you looked."

"How you know that?"

"Because you came back."

"You know where it is?"

"I might."

"You smart, you'll tell me now. You dumb, you'll tell me soon enough." King took another step toward me. He was so close I could see the pulsing of the veins in his massive neck.

"Look, man, either way, you're gonna kill me, right? If that's so, I'm gonna keep the secret to myself."

"Naw. You won't. I'll squeeze it out of you. Like toothpaste from a tube."

I'm a fool. But I figured if I was going to die, I wanted to at least leave a mark, so I stepped in close to George and swung my good hand at his face with all my might. A long, curving roundhouse of a punch that caught him right on the side of his nose. "That was for ChooChoo," I said.

King George's tongue came out and tasted the blood flowing out of his nose and over his lips. He let it flow, doing nothing to wipe it off. He crouched lower and began backing me into a corner of the shop. I looked around for a weapon. There was nothing but clocks. I grabbed a small, heavy mantle clock off a shelf and threw it at King George. He batted it away with his hand and took another step my direction. I grabbed at a six-foot grandfather clock and tipped it toward him. It crashed at his feet, the sound of shattering glass and clanging gongs breaking through the night.

I pulled another clock from the wall and was about to throw it at George, when I realized it was the Hermle. I raised it above my head.

"This doing you no good, Seth," growled George. "I'm-a kill you just the same."

I smashed the Hermle at my own feet. The glass shattered. The wood case broke open. Laying among the pieces was a familiar square of crumpled, yellowed paper. The map. My hand darted down and picked it up.

"You didn't think to look inside the clocks."

He froze. The only part of George that moved was his eyes. They followed every movement of my hand.

"I swear to you," I said, "I will tear this thing in pieces if you take another step toward me. I will tear it to shreds."

"And I'll tear *you* to shreds." He called me a twelve-letter name.

"Kill me. But you'll get nothing for it. Or next to nothing."

He stepped toward me, but when I motioned to tear the map, he backed away. He frowned at me, then his shoulders slumped. "How much you want in on it? I'll give you five percent. A finder's fee. Fifty thou go a long way for a kid like you."

"You're a kid, too, George. And you'd never pay me a dime."

"Just tell me what you want. We can work something out."

While he was talking I saw Carlyle's car pull up outside. George saw it, too. I watched the truth of it form in his eyes. "I'll tell you what I want," I said, "just as soon as I figure it out."

George turned to face the front door. He reached inside his jacket. Carlyle kicked open the door and shot King George in the chest.

Twenty-seven

Once I found out about the map, I had this idea that I'd recover it and personally take it to Azura's house. Two possible scenarios would happen from there. The first was that the Lears would offer me half a million dollars for recovering their heirloom. I'd take it. I could use the money. Who couldn't use an extra half a mil?

The second scenario was that Mr. Lear would offer me a bunch of money and I'd turn it down. I could never figure a really good reason why I would do this, other than some artificial logic about being a white knight—being clean in a dirty world. But nobody's clean. I'm not. The point may be more about trying than succeeding. That's all I can figure.

Neither of these scenarios played out. Carlyle's shot just missed King George's heart. George lived. He'll go to trial eventually. Carlyle said they'd probably try George as an adult. The map was taken by the cops as evidence. Someday they'll give it back to Lear. Like he needs more valuables.

Around noon the next day, I returned to Nadel's shop. The front and back entrances were covered in police tape, but the only real barrier to the back door was a lock and I still had a key. I let myself in and found the Lear clock. It worked perfectly now. It was never broken. I packed it up in its original cardboard box and left.

I figured this clock was my best chance to gain access to Azura. Back in her hospital room, I'd told her it was better if we stayed apart until this whole mess was cleaned up, but she'd been weighing heavy on my heart the whole time. Now that Nadel was dead and George was arrested, I could get back to what mattered.

While I drove Mom's Jeep toward her home, I thought about our chance for a future together. So what if we were from different neighborhoods? We were still from the same city. We both felt pain. We both felt joy. Just maybe we were both in love.

I was strangely nervous when I parked in the Lear driveway. I checked my face in the mirror, then carried the clock onto the porch. The Latino maid answered. She looked kinder than the last time I saw her. "Yes?"

"Your clock. Remember?"

"*Si.* Yes. *Gracias.* Do we owe you anything?"

I smirked. I can't help smirking. "Probably not. Is Azura home?"

"Yes. She went home."

I frowned.

"To California. She went home to California. To her momma."

"Really?"

"Yes. Is good, no?"

I stood there without speaking, then finally nodded and left.

I went to Guinevere's and ordered a cappuccino to go from a male barista, speaking as few words as possible. Nikki came up behind me, with a dishrag in her hand. "'Sup, studly?"

"Nothing much."

"When you coming back to school?"

"Supposedly Monday. Or never."

"You sad again? The only time I've seen you come in here with a smile on your face was when you were with your rich girlfriend."

"She's gone."

Nikki said nothing, but I guess the look on her face had some sympathy in it. At least a little.

I said, "I just found out she went to live with her broke mom in California."

"Really? Dang. Too bad Mom didn't live in Tacoma. Take the money away and that rich girl could have been just what you needed."

She could have been. She probably was. "I thought *you* were just what I needed," I said.

"I *am* what you need, Seth." Nikki twisted her dishrag in her hands. "But I'm not sure you're what I need." She stood on her tiptoes, brushed my cheek with her perfect lips, then disappeared behind the counter.

I delivered the cappuccino to the hospital, but ChooChoo was asleep when I got there. I set the drink on the table next to his bed, knowing that by the time he awoke, the foam would be dead and the coffee would be cold.

I drove the few blocks between the hospital and Shotgun Shack. Shantay wrote down the details of my meal with a smile—fried chicken, red beans, dirty rice. She seemed like a decent waitress, after all.

"That Seth?" shouted Miss Irene from the kitchen, when she heard my voice. "Slugger, come on back here and help me fill an order or two."

I walked into the kitchen, into the spatters of hot oil, the spills of flour. I washed my hands and set to work.

To receive a free catalog of Poisoned Pen Press titles, please provide your name and address through one of the following ways:

Phone: 1-800-421-3976
Facsimile: 1-480-949-1707
Email: info@poisonedpenpress.com
Website: www.poisonedpenpress.com

Poisoned Pen Press / The Poisoned Pencil
6962 E. First Ave. Ste 103
Scottsdale, AZ 85251

CPSIA information can be obtained at www.ICGtesting.com
Printed in the USA
BVOW05n2340300615

406731BV00001BB/2/P